I0459209

Triangles

2

NIA RICH

Also by Nia Rich

Never Going Back

My Love Is Deeper

F**k Boy

Lovers Remorse

Seduced by a Savage

Triangles 2

Written by: Nia Rich
Copyright © 2017 Nia Rich

All rights reserved.

Cover: Tina Louise
Edited by: Venitia Crawford-Fergus

This is a work of fiction. Names, characters, places are either the product of the authors imagination or are used fictitiously and any resemblance to actual persons, living or dead, business establishments, events, or locals, is entirely coincidental.

Triangles

2

Previously in Triangles…

Raelyn

I hung out with Paris and Laron and again; he took us on a movie and dinner date. Paris was still giving me the same energy she had the night we had dinner at their place. She was still smiling and being polite, so I ignored it.

The next weekend they invited me to the theater to see a stage play that was in town. I was going to turn down the offer because of the way I felt about Paris, but I decided to give it one more try and if I wasn't feeling it that time, I was going to back out of the situation.

Laron was a perfect gentleman as usual, and Paris seemed a bit more open with the idea of the three of us. The play was amazing, and I enjoyed myself. As we were walking out of the theater Paris said, "I want to have a real drink. Those drinks in there were weak."

I laughed and said, "Yes they were."

"We should stop in this restaurant before we go home." Paris said.

"You cool with that?" Laron asked me.

"Yea."

"Aight." Laron said.

My legs were freezing as we walked down the street from the theater to the restaurant. It was ten degrees outside and I was wearing a dress and some boots. Paris was wearing the same thing, so I was sure that her legs were cold too. I should have worn jeans, but I was trying to be dressed up for the theater. Paris walked next to me and not next to him which was a change. We sat down at an empty booth. She sat next to me. I started to feel like she was keeping her enemy closer.

"You two look beautiful tonight, but I know that y'all cold in those dresses." Laron said.

We laughed and then Paris said, "Yes we are."

"So, what are we drinking bartender?" Paris asked me.

"Well, what do you like?" I asked.

"You're the professional. Give us your best recommendation." she said.

"You seem like a martini type and he is the Hennessy and coke type."

"Good observation." she said.

"Thank you. Have you ever tried a lemon drop martini? It's my favorite." I said.

"No, but I will tonight." she said.

We ordered our drinks when the waiter made it over to our table.

Paris asked, "Did you enjoy the play?"

I said, "Very much so."

"I saw you over there laughing at some parts." she said.

"I was." I said.

Paris smiled and looked up when the waiter returned with our drinks. She thanked the waiter and took a sip of her lemon drop martini, and then she said, "Mmmm. This is good. You were right. I do like this."

I smiled and took a sip of my drink.

"I see you know your stuff." Paris said.

"I do." I said.

"That's going to be your new favorite drink baby." Laron said.

"It really is babe." Paris said as she took another sip. Laron laughed, and I smiled. He and I caught eye contact from across the table and I felt tingles. She looked at him and then at me. I broke eye contact with him and pulled my cell phone out of my pocket. I got a text message from my sister that said to call her. I made a mental note to make sure I called her after the date. I put my phone back into my handbag. I decided to ask some questions.

"Do you have siblings back in California?" I asked Paris.

Paris replied, "Yes. I have an older brother and sister."

"Do you ever go home to visit your family?"

"All the time. Do you have siblings?" she asked.

"Yes, I have a twin sister and an older brother."

"You have a twin?"

"Yes. I thought you knew?" I laughed.

"You didn't tell me she had a twin." Paris said to Laron.

"I thought you knew babe. I showed you her social media profile."

"I looked but I didn't see any pics of you and your twin."

"Oh, yea because most of my profile pics are just of me. The pics of me and her are in my timeline photos."

Paris said, "Oh ok. Well, I wasn't digging that hard. I wasn't trying to be a creeper you know. I was just trying to see what you looked like."

I laughed. Seemed like the liquor was loosening her up a little. We chatted about family for a little while longer and then I excused myself to the bathroom.

"Excuse me. I am going to go to the ladies' room." I said.

"Ok." Laron said.

"I'll come with you." Paris said. She slid out of the booth first and then I slid out. She stopped to give Laron a kiss while I was adjusting my dress. We chatted about not falling in our heels on the way to the restroom. After we used the bathroom, we stood at the mirror to refresh our make-up.

Paris asked, "How does it feel to be a twin?"

"Sometimes it feels like I'm fighting for my own identity, but I love it. I truly have a best friend for life.

"That's really special."

"Thanks"

"You know. You seem really cool." she said.

I looked at Paris through the mirror and said, "Are you sure? Because I was under the impression that you didn't like me."

"Did I come off like that?" she asked.

"Um hum." I said while applying more lipstick.

"It wasn't like that. I was just feeling a little uncomfortable." Paris said looking back at me through our reflections in the mirror.

"Why?" I asked.

She turned to face me and said, "Woman to woman. I just hoping that you didn't plan to come and try to steal my husband."

"Steal your husband? Y'all invited me in." I chuckled.

Her mentioning her worries about her husband being taken made me wonder if she knew that her husband told me that he loved me several times, and I wondered if she knew that he had given me the best head ever a couple times. I kept it to myself. It wasn't my business to tell. He said they were open with each other about everything, so she had to know.

Paris said, "I know, but my husband orchestrated the whole thing and he was spending a lot of time with you,

I was hoping that we were all on the same page you know?"

"I understand, and I don't want to steal anyone. This is new for me too."

"Seems like you really like my husband."

"I do." I said.

"I can tell that he really likes you too." she said.

"Yea we have good chemistry, but I am not trying to steal him. I knew what it was when I made the decision to move forward."

Paris nodded her head and then she asked, "So, are you a lesbian?"

"No, are you?"

"No."

Both of us laughed.

"Like I said, I'm just trying something new." I said.

"Me to girl."

"So, are we cool now?" I asked.

"Yes." Paris smiled at me. I smiled back and we left the bathroom.

Laron stood up to greet us when we made It back to the table. He kissed her on the lips and then he kissed me on the cheek.

"What happened in the bathroom that made you two come back smiling?"

"Nothing." We said at the same time and then we laughed.

"Uh-huh. Something happened." he laughed.

"Nothing happened baby." Paris said. She stood up and sat next to him. She kissed him again.

"Ok." Jamir said. He looked over at the bar and said, "There goes my boy Jamir. Excuse me ladies. I'll be right back." He stood up and walked over to Jamir who was standing at the bar by himself.

"Do you know him?" she whispered from across the table.

"Yea. He talks to my sister."

"Your twin?"

"Um hum."

"I don't like him."

"Tell your sister to be careful. He is a hoe. I hate when my husband hangs with him." She whispered. We noticed that Laron was walking back over to the table with Jamir, so we cut the conversation.

"Ladies you know Jamir, right?" Laron asked. Both of us nodded and said hello to him.

"Aight my dude. I got to break out. It was good seeing you ladies." Jamir slapped hands with Laron and walked away. I could have sworn I saw some girl meet him at the door, but he turned her around and they left.

"You know that I don't like him." Paris said to Laron.

"I know baby, but that's my boy." Laron said. He walked over to my side of the table and then he looked at Paris and asked, "Do you mind?"

"No." she said.

He sat down next to me. "Are you enjoying yourself?" he asked me.

"Yes."

"Good." he said kissing my cheek afterwards.

"Do you ladies want another round?"

"Sure." I said. Paris nodded her head. Laron signaled for the waitress to come back to our table. He ordered another round of drinks for us.

After the second round of drinks all of us were loose, joking, and laughing. Paris seemed more open and free. I felt more comfortable around the two of them. I was having blast. The two of them together were a riot. There wasn't as much tension as there was the first couple times we hung out.

"Aight, fuck it. I want to see you two kiss." Paris said loosely. I could tell that she was feeling the liquor a little bit.

"Are you sure?" Laron asked.

"Um hum." Paris said after swallowing down the last of her second drink. Laron smiled and then he pulled my chin to him and gave me a passionate kiss with a lot of tongue.

"Dang, you don't kiss me like that babe." she said.

"Yes, I do. Stop it." Laron chuckled.

I laughed and wiped the left-over wetness from my lips. He stood up and sat next to her and kissed her the same way that he kissed me. I knew that I was feeling the liquor because I was a little turned on by it. When they finished kissing, Paris smiled at me. I smiled back and said, "You two make a cute couple."

"Thank you." she said. "I'm not going to lie; you and my husband look good together too."

"You think so?" I asked.

"Um hum." she responded and then she told Laron to order some more drinks.

By time the third drink was finished, Paris was sitting next to me with her hand on my leg. We were giggling and talking about nothing that was important. Halfway through the fourth drink, I was gone and way beyond my limit. Paris was past her drinking limit too. She told me that she thought that I was beautiful and then she kissed me. It was a peck but it was enough for all of us to know that the boundaries had been crossed.

Laron paid the bill and we headed out. When I stood up, I almost stumbled and Paris caught me. We laughed about it while standing at the door waiting for

Laron to pull up with their car. When he arrived, Paris climbed into the back seat with me. That first kiss at the table opened the door because she came right at me for a second one as soon as she closed the car door, and then suddenly, we couldn't stop kissing each other. It was so steamy in the back seat with her and I that Laron could barely keep his eyes on the road while driving back to their house.

When we made it to their house, Paris held my hand and walked me upstairs to their bedroom and Laron followed us. I was too gone to even care about what I was doing.

"Y'all go ahead I just want to watch for a minute." he said.

Both of us took off out boots and dresses and then we began kissing again. Her lips were softer than Laron's and her kiss was more erotic. I had never kissed a girl in my life and kissing her was better than any kiss that I'd ever had. We tasted each other's tongues while Laron stood behind us watching. She put her soft manicured hand on my breast and rubbed one of my hardened nipples as we kissed, and then I did the same to her. She reached behind me to unhook my bra. Once mine was off, I took off hers.

We stopped to examine each other's bodies. Mine, chocolate brown, and athletic. Hers, peanut butter, slim, and soft. My breasts a little smaller than hers. My areola circles and nipples much darker than her shade of tan.

"You are beautiful." she whispered.

"So are you." I responded.

"She is gorgeous babe." She smiled at Laron.

He said, "I know."

Paris stepped back to me, pressed her hard nipples up against mine and started kissing me again. Laron undressed down to his boxers and then he approached us and joined in the kiss. The three of us tasted each other's tongues and lips and then she watched Laron kiss me for a few seconds before putting one of my breasts in her mouth. I felt like I was floating. I had never been kissed and had my nipples sucked on at the same time.

"Lay down." he whispered to me. After I laid down, he said to Paris, "Taste her."

She did what he asked. Paris crawled onto the bed and put her soft lips on my box ever so gently. She kissed it a few times and then used two fingers to separate my lips.

She wrapped her soft, tan colored lips around my pearl, sucked on it softly, and then she slowly and gently rubbed and flicked her tongue on it.

"Mmmm." I moaned out loud. Her head game was better than her husbands.

"That's right." Laron said when he heard me moaning. He watched for a moment and then he bent down and helped his wife give me oral pleasure. They licked and sucked on me together. I watched them take turns on me and then they began flicking their tongues on my pearl at the same time. I grabbed the sheets and moaned obscenities to the ceiling. Laron let Paris take over and then he stood up and told Paris that she looked sexy as hell.

"That's right. Do it like that. Stay on it." he said.

Laron walked behind her and smacked her ass. She got onto her knees and he pushed his tool inside her from behind. He kept his eyes on her licking me while he deep stroked his wife. She whined a little when he hit the right spot. Laron leaned forward so he could help her taste me again. I felt my O and then I heard her moan that she was about to cum. My back arched when I got mine.

"Ah!" I moaned loudly towards the ceiling.

"Baby I'm cuming!" she yelled.

My body froze for a few seconds, and hers shook a little. Laron started kissing her as she was feeling the aftershock from her orgasm.

"This is so sexy." Paris whispered to him.

"I know." he whispered back.

Laron pulled out of her, put a condom on, and then he climbed on top of me. He stared into my eyes first before he entered me. This was going to be our first time making love to each other. Although his wife was right there in the room with us, for that moment, it felt like it was just me and him. Laron leaned down to kiss me. He took his time going in. It was like he wanted me to feel every inch of him, or maybe he wanted to feel all of me. I moaned when I felt his thickness slide inside of me. I did not know that he was working with all that. A purring sound escaped from my lips as he grinded his manhood into me in slow circular motion. Once he was all the way in, he stayed deep inside using his tool to search for my G spot. Paris laid on the side of me watching her husband make love to me. She looked just as shocked as I felt that it was all happening.

Laron looked at Paris and said, "Come here baby."

She crawled over to him and kissed him and then she came to me and put one of my breasts into her mouth. He smacked her on the ass and told her to put it on my face. Paris crawled up to my face and placed her peach on my lips. She was facing the wall and holding on to the headboard. She slightly grinded her hips on to my face. I tasted her sweetness. I listened to her sounds. Her moans made me feel like I was doing it right, so I kept at it.

Paris looked down at me and whispered, "Yes, right there."

"Get it baby." he said. Laron knew his wife's sounds and he could tell that she was about to cum.

Paris screamed out, "Ah!"

She creamed on my lips, and then she crawled off me and tasted her essence from my lips. Laron pulled out of me and laid down on his back. He told his wife to get on top of him and he told me to climb onto his face. Paris and I were both riding him, and he was giving us both pleasure at the same time. I looked down at him and watched him eat my peach. He was slurping and licking like it was his last meal. I spread my lips a little wider for him to get to my center. I began grinding my hips and moaning louder. I could hear Paris bouncing on him and moaning louder too. The sounds and the feeling put me in a zone. I grabbed the headboard and started going for mine. Laron smacked my ass. That boosted my adrenaline. I started talking to him and telling him how good it felt and to not stop. I felt Paris tap my ass a couple of times, and then I lost control. My orgasm rocked my body. I screeched a couple of obscenities before rolling off his face onto the bed next to him. I had my eyes closed while trying to get myself back together. I heard Paris moan that another orgasm was coming. I heard her hit a high note, so I opened my eyes and looked at them. They looked sexy making love to each other. Her body was limp from her orgasm, but Laron was gripping her waist and pounding upwards into her. She had her hands on his chest, and he was telling her to tell him that she loved it.

"I love it." Paris said.

Laron made a deep growl like sound and then he busted into her. Paris rolled off him onto the bed on the other side of him. When it was all over, the sun was coming up, and we passed out in the bed together. It was done. I had had my first threesome with Laron and his wife.

Nia Rich

Triangles

2

NIA RICH

"I don't care what anybody says. Love triangles are not cool no matter which way you slice them up." - Cherry

Chapter 1

Raelyn

When I woke up, it was late morning; early afternoon. I was still in bed with Paris. Laron had already gotten out of bed. I rubbed my eyes and felt a slight headache forming. The morning sun shining through the window felt extremely bright. I put my arm above my face to block the sunlight.

"Good morning." Laron said quietly when he walked into the room. He kissed me and said, "I was just coming to wake you two up. I cooked breakfast and I set out some towels and a toothbrush for you so that you can get freshened up."

"Ok. What time is it?" I whispered.

"It's almost eleven o'clock."

"Oh man. I got to get home." I said. I was running late to meet my sister for the gym. I searched the room for my purse and then I saw it on the dresser.

"Can you hand me my purse?" I asked.

"Yup." Laron said.

He walked over to the dresser, picked up my purse, and handed it to me. He kissed me again and then he walked over to Paris to wake her up. I opened my purse and pulled my phone out. I sent a text message to my sister to tell her that I was not going to make it. I wrapped myself in their bed blanket and walked to the bathroom. I took a shower, brushed my teeth, and I put my hair into a bun. I put the dress back on that I had on the night before and I put my panties into my purse. My sister always told me that when you return home in the clothes that you wore the night before, you would be taking the walk of shame from your car to your house. I chuckled at my reflection in the mirror. "The walk of shame it is." I said to myself.

When I walked down stairs to the kitchen, Paris was already down there. She had taken a shower in their second bathroom and was sitting at the table eating.

"Good morning." Paris said when I approached the table. I sat down and said the same to her.

"How are you feeling." she asked.

I said, "I have a headache. You?"

"Same."

We chuckled a little.

"Last night was so sexy by the way." Paris smiled at me.

"Yes, it was." I said and smiled at her.

I took a couple bites of the food, but I had no appetite. I was too hung over. I excused myself from breakfast and told them that I needed to get home. Paris hugged me and Laron walked me to my car.

Frigid air made me shiver when I stepped outside of their house. The glare from the sun was blinding and made my headache even stronger. I pushed the button on my key ring to start my car. Laron and I stopped walking at my driver side door. He wrapped his arms around my neck and gave me a kiss.

After the kiss, he said, "You know that I enjoyed last night, right?"

"Did you?"

"Absolutely."

"Did you?" he asked.

"I did." I smiled.

"It's not over, so don't try to run off."

"I'm not." I laughed.

"You still coming to Vegas with us, right?"

"Yes."

"Alright. It's cold out here, so I'll let you go. I am going to call you a little later." he said. He opened my car door for me to get in. I pulled off and headed home.

***

I took the walk of shame when I got to my apartment building. I was glad that I could park in the underground parking garage. I prayed that no one would see me walking into the building with the clothes I left out in the night before. I walked quickly into my building and took the stairs up to my third-floor apartment. I walked hurriedly down the hall and slid into my apartment after locking the door.

"Whew." I said out loud.

There wasn't anyone in the garage or hallway of my apartment building. I walked into my room and plopped down onto my bed. I laid back and on my bed and looked up at the ceiling. I thought about what had just gone down the night before with Laron and Paris. I shook my head back and forth. I couldn't believe that I had had a threesome with my lover and his wife. I never in my life thought that I would have a threesome, and with a married couple at that. I closed my eyes and images of them tasting me together filled my mind. I started to feel tingles throughout my body and then a smile spread across my face. I thought that I would feel weird after doing it, but I felt no regret at all. Having sex with the two of them had put my vibrators to shame. Especially Laron. He was working with something and he knew how to work with it. He was just as skilled with his tool as he was with his tongue. I understood why Paris was worried about some chick coming along to steal her husband. She wasn't bad in bed either. Although it was her first time as well, she handled me like a professional.

I sat up in bed and said, "That shit was crazy!" I laughed.

I stood up and walked to my bedroom closet. I removed my dress and I took my panties out of my purse. I put them both in my dirty clothes hamper. I walked over to my dresser and pulled out a pair of pajamas. I put on my pajamas and slid my feet into my slippers and walked to my kitchen to hook up some breakfast to nurse my slight hangover. I responded to a text message from my sister and then I got a text message from Laron.

Hey beautiful. We enjoyed you last night. I know that you know that I enjoyed you more. The whole experience still feels like a dream. I can't stop thinking about it. I loved how you tasted, how you felt, your sex faces, sounds you made. Thank you for stepping outside of your box and trying something new. It's not over yet. Vegas baby.

I smiled and read the message again as I poured a half a glass of champagne and then filled the rest of the glass with orange juice. I put my phone down on the counter. I sipped on my mimosa while scrambling some eggs. I sprinkled a little shredded cheese on my eggs and lowered a couple of pieces of multigrain bread into my toaster. When they popped up I spread a little strawberry jam across them, set them on the plate next to my eggs, and walked with my plate in hand to my dining room table. I sat down and sent Laron a reply message.

Thank you for an amazing evening. I haven't gotten over it either. I enjoyed you both more than you know. I can't wait to get to Las Vegas.

After I sent the message, I got a message from my sister telling me that she would call me later.

***

I hooked up with Taji later that afternoon for lunch. I hadn't seen her in a while and I wanted to catch up. I was itching to share my news with someone, but my sister was busy. She said that she was trying to get some homework done, so I called Taji.

"So, what's been up with you? You've been M.I.A lately." Taji said.

I laughed "No I haven't."

"Girl yes you have. I barely see you anymore, and you only communicate mostly through text message. What's up with that?" Taji asked.

"I am sorry girl. You know I've been all caught up with Laron."

"That guy that you've been dating?"

"Um hum."

"I ain't trying to be all in your business or nothing, but I heard that he was married."

"He is, and um." I made a bashful face.

"What?"

"I am kind of dating both."

"Laron and his wife?!"

"Shhhh." I said as I looked around the restaurant.

"I don't want the entire world to know. Just my girls."

"Oh my God girl! You didn't tell me that! Are you having sex with them too?"

"Um, yea. I did."

"Shut up girl!"

"It's true."

"When!?"

"Last night."

"What! Wow. Rae. I didn't know you had it in you girl. You are a certified freak now."

"No, I am not. I am just trying something new. I guess you can say I am experimenting."

"I can't believe you."

"I know. I can't believe myself. I actually liked it."

"Wow. Well, welcome to my world."

"Your freaky ass ain't got nothing going on."

"Not much anymore but arguing with my man all the time. I am so sick and tired of him lying to me."

"I feel you."

"Truth be told, I've been seeing someone else."

"What? Nah girl."

"Yep."

"How is that going to help?"

"It's not, but it makes me feel good."

"I hear you girl."

"Well anyways. Was it good?"

"Hell yea."

"Did she eat your box?"

"Hell yea, they ate my box at the same time. It was sexy Taji."

"Damnnnn."

"I know right."

"I am jealous."

I laughed and took a sip of my drink.

"Would you do it again?"

"Girl again, and again, and again." I laughed.

Taji laughed and said, "Shoot. I don't blame you. You have got to keep me updated on your situation and I want all the juicy details."

"You know that I will."

Triangles 2

Chapter 2

Paris

Up until that night, I hadn't been with a woman, nor was I interested in having a sexual encounter with a female. I agreed to bringing another woman into the bedroom to please my husband. I never thought that I would hear myself say that being with a woman wasn't bad at all. Having the threesome with Raelyn and my husband was the sexiest sexual experience that I'd ever had. I thought that I was going to feel some type of way about seeing my husband make love to another woman, but I was turned on by it. The way he handled both of us excited me, and the whole experience made my husband and I even more attracted to each other. After Raelyn left the next morning, my husband and I made love like some animals.

I had to hook up with my best friend and tell her about what happened. I stopped over her house in Maple Grove early afternoon. She was happy to see me and greeted me with a hug when she opened the door. I followed her into her place.

"What's been up?" Priscilla asked as I sat down at her dining room table with her. She poured me a glass of wine out of the bottle she had already opened. She put the bottle down and picked up her glass.

"Oh, nothing much except Laron and I having a threesome."

"What?" she asked and put down her glass.

"Yes" I smiled.

"When?"

"The other night." I said. I picked up my glass and took a sip.

"With the girl that you were telling me about?"

"Yes."

"I can't believe you did it." she said as she shook her head back and forth. Priscilla picked her glass back up.

"I can't believe that I did it either." I said.

"How was it? Did you like it?"

"It was amazing. I loved it." I said after taking a sip of the wine.

"Did you eat her?"

"Yes."

"Oh, my God."

"I know."

"Was it nasty?"

"No. It was sexy."

"Did your husband have sex with her?"

"Yes."

"And you weren't uncomfortable?"

"Surprisingly, I wasn't."

"Damn girl. You're a good one. I couldn't do it. Especially not with another female." she said and took a sip of her wine.

"I thought you said that you had a threesome?"

"I did, but I didn't touch her."

"You don't know what you're missing."

"Nothing. Because I'm not with it." she said. I laughed and swallowed down some more wine.

"It made us more attracted to each other. We've been having sex non-stop since that night. He keeps talking about how he loved seeing me taste her box."

"Wow. Oh my God. What if she tries to take your man girl?"

"She can't. What me and Laron have is solid, and too, she knows what it is. I've already had a woman to woman with her."

"What did you say?"

"I just told her that it wasn't going down like that." I said. Priscilla laughed.

"Would you do it again?"

"Yea. Actually, we are going to Vegas this weekend together."

"So, do you like girls now?"

"No. I am just open to the experience with my husband."

"Um hum. Open to doing anything for him."

I laughed. "Whatever."

***

I headed back home after I hung out with Pricilla for a while. My husband wrapped his arms around me and kissed me as soon as I walked in the door.

"Hey baby!" he said cheerfully.

I giggled and said, "Hey babe!"

"Where did you and Priscilla go?"

"Nowhere. We just hung out at her house."

"Ok," he said as he closed the door. "Let me take your coat. I made you dinner."

I smiled. "You made me dinner tonight? What is the occasion?"

"I just wanted to do something for my beautiful, sexy, wife to thank her for the wonderful time I had with her the other night. Thank you, baby."

I smiled, kissed him, and said, "I love you."

"I love you more baby." he said.

I removed my boots and put them on the mat by our shoe rack. I followed my husband through our house to the kitchen to see what he cooked.

"Mmm it smells good in here." I said as I lifted the top of one of the pots.

I turned on the sink water and washed my hands. I used a paper towel to dry them and then I followed my husband to the dining room table. He pulled out my chair for me to sit down, poured red wine into my glass, and set a plate of food in front of me. He turned and walked back into the kitchen and came back with a plate of food for himself. He sat down across the table from me.

He said, "Let's toast." We lifted our glasses. "To us and to everlasting love."

We clinked out glasses together and took sips of our wine.

"When we are done eating, I plan to bath you, rub you down with some oil, and make love to you."

My smile had not left my face since I walked in the door. If I had known that having a threesome was going to bring all this romance out of him, I would have done it sooner. I took another sip from the red wine in my glass and then I took a bite of my food.

"Baby this is delicious." I said with a mouth full of food.

"I made it with love." he replied.

"Thank you for all this baby." I said.

"You don't have to thank me wife. You deserve it,"

I smiled and then he asked me, "Now that a few days have gone by, how do you feel about it now?"

"I still feel like it was one of the sexiest experiences I have ever had in my life. I loved every minute of it. You were doing your thing baby. It turned me on to see you handle both of us like that."

"You did your thing too, woman. I didn't know that you had it in you. You looked good as hell eating her box, and the faces you were making when she was eating yours. Damn girl!"

I giggled.

"I'm serious. You should have seen my view. When she was on your face though. Oooo wee."

I giggled again and said, "Yea the whole thing was hot."

"Yes, it was. Are you ready for Vegas?"

"More than ready."

"I can't wait."

Chapter 3

Raelyn

"Yo!" I said when I opened the door for Riley.

I hugged her and moved back, so she could walk in. She took her boots off at the door and hung her coat on the back of my dining room chair.

"You need a coat rack."

"Shut up. Don't come in my place trying to interior decorate."

"I'm just saying."

"Whatever."

"Are you ready to watch this Empire?"

"You know it. I got our popcorn and candy. Would you like a shot of Patron?"

"Yes." she said.

We couldn't wait to watch Empire. It was one of our favorite television series and the new season was premiering. Riley had shown up early as usual which was great because we had some time to talk before the television show came on. I poured us both a shot over some ice in separate glasses and walked over to the couch where she was sitting. I handed her a glass and sat down next to her. The television was already rested on the channel the program would be showing on.

"What's wrong?" I asked when I leaned back on the couch. I knew something was wrong. I know my twin. Her energy was off again.

"Jamir." she said.

"What happened?"

"He walked out on me the other night and I haven't heard from him since. I've tried calling him several times, but he won't answer my calls."

"Why?"

"I don't know. We sort of got into an argument at my place the other night because I asked him where we were in the relationship."

"What did he say?"

"He said that we were just chilling right now and trying to build, and I'm like how long is this building supposed to happen?"

"Right."

"For real sister. I mean it's been like six months. A man should know if he wants to be with a woman by now. He told me that I was being dramatic and left." Riley said. I saw water fill her eyes.

"Aww sister don't cry."

"I'm sorry. I'm just so frustrated."

I put my glass down and moved closer to her and hugged her. I held her in my arms and let her cry on my shoulder.

"I really like him."

"I know Ri but he's a jerk and you don't deserve that."

She lifted her head from my shoulder and wiped some more tears. I stood up and got some Kleenex and used it to dab her tears. I wanted to tell her what Paris had told me about him the other night, and that I think I saw him with another chick, but I didn't want to make her feel worse.

"I guess I just had hope you know."

"I know, but there are other guys out there."

"I'm just tired of looking. I wanted him to be the one." she exhaled loudly.

"Anyways. Enough of my sob story. What's up with you? I called you that night, but you didn't answer. Riley said.

She pulled another piece of Kleenex out of the box I had in my hand and wiped the rest of her tears. I put the box of Kleenex down and picked my glass back up.

"Um, about that night." I said with a smirk on my face.

"What about it?"

"Let's just say, my two-year sex drought is over."

"What!" she yelled.

"Yes." I smiled.

"Get out of here! With him!?"

"With them both."

"No way."

"Um hum."

"But, I thought that you said she didn't like you?"

"All that changed that night."

"Oh, my gosh Rae, you are crazy!"

I laughed and leaned back on the couch.

Riley asked, "Did you do her?"

"Yes, and she did me, and he did me, and I did him, and they did each other."

"Sister!"

"What?"

"I can't believe you." she said while shaking her head back and forth, and then she asked, "What was it like?"

"It was four of the most amazing orgasms that I've ever had in my life. Those two put my vibrators to shame." I said and then we laughed.

Riley shook her head and said, "I can't believe you."

"Believe it. I kissed a girl and I liked it."

"Ew. I could never do a girl."

"It was unbelievable. Oh, and Laron? Sister, Laron puts it down! He handles his business in the bedroom." I said and smiled.

"Damn."

"That's what I said."

"So, now what? Are you done?"

"We are going to Vegas this weekend."

"So, you're basically dating a couple now. That's crazy sister. Who does that?"

"Me." I said. I picked up my drink and took a sip.

Nia Rich

Chapter 4

Riley

Riley chilled with her sister a little while after the show Empire went off. They talked about how the episode went. They also talked about their brother Eazy's newest baby mama drama. They can't stand his baby's mother. Back in the days' when he first got with her, they'd heard that she was a hoe, but he was so in love that he couldn't see it. Fast forward years later, and there is all kind of drama between them. Most times they wish that Eazy would have listened to them instead of getting the chick pregnant.

As Riley sat in her car waiting for it to warm up, she thought about what her sister Raelyn had told her. She was shocked to find out that her sister went all the way with the married couple. Raelyn was never the wild and crazy type, so it was not like her to do something like that. Riley's phone began vibrating in her middle console and broke her thoughts about her sister. She picked it up and saw Jamir's name and number. Riley answered it fast. She didn't want to miss that call because she didn't know if he would call her again.

"Hello?"

"What's up Riley?"

"You tell me. You've been the one missing."

"I know and I miss you. I want to see you."

"Why? You walked out on me and I haven't heard from you since."

"I know. I'm sorry. I had a lot of things on my mind, but I miss you."

Riley rubbed her hand across her forehead and bit her bottom lip. She knew that she should have been cursing him out and hanging up the phone, but she couldn't pull herself to do it.

Riley said, "I miss you too Jamir."

"Can I see you?"

**

"You like that?" Jamir whispered into Riley's ear.

"Yes." Riley moaned.

Jamir had only been at Riley's apartment for three minutes before they were butt naked in her bed. He was on top of her, chest to chest, and he had his head rested on her shoulder. Riley had her legs wrapped around his waist and her hands on the headboard above their heads. She was trying to stop the headboard from knocking up against the wall, but it wasn't working. Riley made a mental note to rearrange her room like she was supposed to do already. She knew her neighbors were probably pissed. They had been at it for a while and Jamir wasn't stopping. He lifted and pushed her legs back as far as they could go as he continued to pound into her. Jamir was going in on Riley and she was on the verge of tapping out. She bit her bottom lip as she felt each thrust.

Riley moaned, "I can't"

"Can't what?"

"I can't take it."

"Oh, you done?"

"Yea." she moaned.

"Nah, you ain't done. Take this dick." Jamir said. He pounded even harder and Riley squealed, "Ahhh shit!"

She let go of the headboard and covered her mouth with her hands to muffle her loud moans and squeals. Jamir didn't say anything else. He was focused on what he was doing.

"Jamir." Riley moaned breathlessly.

"Hum?" he replied

"Stop." she moaned.

"Uh-uh."

"Jamir." she moaned again.

He didn't respond, and he didn't stop. He kept going and then right when Riley yelled out, "Fuuuck!" he busted and pulled out of her.

"Oh, my God. Boy, you are crazy." Riley said. She felt like she couldn't move, and her peach was throbbing.

Jamir said, "You know you like it."

"I do." Riley laughed.

Jamir laughed and said, "I missed you."

He kissed Riley and then walked into the bathroom. Riley watched him walked to the bathroom with dreamy eyes and then she smiled and pulled the sheet up to her neck when he closed the door. Riley heard him flush the toilet. She knew that was the condom he was flushing. When Riley heard the shower, she knew that meant that he was leaving. Riley stood up and walked to the bathroom door. She lightly knocked and then slowly opened the door. Jamir was still standing at the sink.

"I guess you're leaving huh?" Riley asked.

"Yea I got to catch a flight in the morning." he said.

Riley nodded her head and walked back into the room.

"Don't look like that. I will be back the day after tomorrow and I will spend the night." he called out from the bathroom.

Riley put her robe on and started changing the sheets on her bed. She was disappointed, but she had gotten used to his shenanigans. *At least he put his A game on with the D.* Riley thought. As she was pulling the sheets off her bed, she noticed that he had left his phone on her nightstand with the face side down. She tip-toed over to it and picked it up, but the phone wasn't on.

"He has his phone face side down and it's off?" she whispered.

Riley started to turn it on, but he heard Jamir turn the shower water off. She swiftly put the cell phone back on the nightstand and walked over to the bed. She threw the sweaty sheets in the hamper. Riley walked across the room and pulled a fresh set of sheets out of the closet. Jamir walked out of the bathroom with a towel wrapped around him. He dried off, dressed, and then Riley walked him to the door. She made a sad face when he walked out.

"Stop that shit." Jamir said. He kissed her and then he said, "I'll see you in a couple of days."

"Ok." Riley said. She closed the door and locked it after Jamir walked off the porch and towards his car, and then Riley walked back upstairs to her place to take a bath.

Chapter 5

Raelyn

Laron rang my doorbell, so I buzzed him in. He walked through my door with a huge bouquet of roses. The expensive kind, not the ones that come from the gas station. A few gifts and a big teddy bear. I smiled big.

"What is all this for?" I asked.

"Because you're beautiful, and to thank you for a wonderful time."

"Awww this is so sweet." I smiled and took the things from him.

We walked over to my couch and sat down so I could open the gifts. I set the teddy bear next to me on the couch, and then I put the vase of flowers on the table. I opened the first square box and it was a pretty gold necklace. The second box had the matching earrings in it.

I smiled and said, "Aww thank you. These are beautiful. I love them."

"I love you." Laron said.

"I love you too." I said.

Laron helped me put the necklace and earring on. As he was doing it, a thought crossed my mind about whether his wife knew that he would tell me that he loved me. I also wondered if she knew that he bought me the gift, but I didn't ask any questions. I didn't want to kill the moment.

"It looks nice on you. I knew that it would."

"Let me see." I said before standing up to walk over to my wall mirror. The necklace had a bunch of shimmery gold tassels hanging that lay flat on my chest and the earrings had the same tassels hanging from them.

"Yes, it's beautiful."

"Just like you." he said from behind me.

He walked over and stood behind me in the mirror. I turned around and hugged him.

"Thank you so much." I said.

"You're welcome you deserve it."

We gave each other a kiss. It was a quick kiss, but then it turned into something more passionate. We closed our eyes and began sharing tongues, and then sucking lips and the next thing I knew he was kissing my chin, and then my collar bone, and as I was tilting my head back to receive more, he put his hand on one of my breast, and then he stopped himself.

"Um. I'm sorry. I guess I got a little carried away."

I said, "Yea. Me too."

I fixed my shirt and then he asked, "How about lunch? We haven't been out in a while."

"Ok." I said.

My kitty was thumping, and my heart was pounding hard and fast. That kiss had sent my hormones into overdrive, and since I had felt him inside me already, I couldn't help but to crave him. I'd thought about that night with him and Paris repeatedly. I had even masturbated to the thought of that night countless times, but my vibrators didn't have nothing on the two of them; especially not Laron. I had to put Laron the toy to rest and start using a different one to get mine off.

I told myself to calm down. I understood the arrangement, but I couldn't help how I felt. I was sure that he wanted me too, but he was trying to respect his marriage and whatever agreement they had.

"Cool let's go. Oh, before I forget. Paris would like to know if you would like to go shopping with her before the Vegas trip. Are you comfortable with that?"

"Sure." I responded.

"Ok. I'll let her know. Is it ok if I give her your number?"

"Yea."

"Ok."

***

"These bathing suits suck." Paris said as we walked through a clothing store at The Mall of America.

"They do."

"They don't have any bling or creative detailing."

"They don't, and the colors are whack."

"I agree."

"If I was thinking, I would have ordered a bathing suit from one of those online stores. They have more options."

"They do."

"Well we can always wait until we get to Vegas. Do you want to get something to eat? I am hungry."

"Yea."

"What are you in the mood for? Food court food or restaurant?"

"Let's do restaurant. I don't want to bulk up before Vegas."

Paris laughed and said, "True!" She gave me a high five as we walked out of the store.

We walked through the enormous mall to the other side. We found a restaurant that had a salad bar. Once we were seated we put the few bags we had in our hands on the ground next to us and ordered waters with lemon slices from the waitress.

"What do you do when you are not at work?" Paris asked me.

"Well I chill, run errands, hang out with my sister. I also like to work out."

"I can tell. Your body is killer." she said.

"Thank you."

"I like working out too. I try to get Laron to come with me. He does sometimes, but he is not consistent. Besides, he has a natural build, where as I have to work on mine."

I laughed. "Seems like men have it so easy. Are you nervous about your runway show?"

"A little. I always get a little case of the stage fright jitters right before I am going to walk a runway."

"What is your biggest fear?" I asked.

"Falling down the runway. These days there are too many cameras around to be rolling down the runway head first."

I laughed and said, "Right. It will be nice to see you in your element."

"Thank you. Are you ready to ditch this snow for some sun and palm trees?"

"Yes I am."

"I know me too. I know my husband is ready for more than just the palm trees."

I giggled. "I bet he is."

"Girl he is. My husband is a man in that aspect."

She laughed and held up her glass of wine. "Here's to a good time in Vegas."

"Cheers."

Chapter 6

Raelyn

Sitting in the salon chair letting Tamika sew my wet and wavy tresses in to my hair for Vegas. I could hear Taji standing outside arguing with her boyfriend about God knows what.

"Damn girl, she is going off." Tamika said.

"I know. She always is."

"Sounds like she needs to break up with him." Anya said when he walked past to walk to the front of the salon.

I said, "I've been told her that, but she doesn't listen to me. I don't know why she wastes her time arguing with him. I would have been done."

"Me too girl." Tamika said.

Taji walked back into the salon with frown on her face. Her boyfriend had her beyond mad.

"I am so sick of him." she said when she sat down in the stylist chair next to mine.

"Girl I don't know why you put up with it." I said.

"I don't know why either. Every time I try to leave, he finds a way to pull me back."

"It must be good dick, or some money to be going through all that." Anya said.

Everyone laughed.

"Shoot I am for real." Anya said as she sat down in his stylist chair."

"I love him, but I am always catching him in a lie about something. This time he was flirting with some chick on Instagram, and I checked him about it. He claims that I was just tripping, but my question was, why in the hell are you putting a bunch of hearts and kissy faces on this stripper chicks post, and why is she referring to you as babe?"

"Oh boy." I said.

"See that kind of stuff is a no, no. My man knows better than that." Tamika said.

"Everybody's man knows better than that besides mine. So, I look through his posts and see that the chick has been commenting on some of his posts too, so I screen shot the post and send it to my friend. She tells me that she knows the chick and she has seen them together." Taji said.

"Oh wow." Tamika said.

"Yea, so I sent the bitch a message and asked her how she knows my man and why she's been on his posts."

"Ha! No, you didn't." Anya said. He was laughing and clapping his hands.

"Yes, I did." Taji said.

"Well, what did she say."

"She said bitch ask your man, so I said bitch I'm asking you!"

"Oooo!" Anya said. He clapped his hands some more. Anya lives for some good drama. He was all in Taiji's story like he was watching a good episode of Love and Hip Hop.

"Did she respond?" Anya asked.

"Yea, she said that she was going to beat my ass, and I told her where to meet me. That bitch don't want none."

"Ahahahaha!" Anya laughed out loud.

"Uh, uh." Tamika said.

"Yea and I guess she called him, so that was him just calling me to cuss me out. Talking about I had no business sending her a message on Instagram."

"Ah. What?" Anya asked.

"Um hum, so I started snapping on him, and that is what y'all heard."

"Shit, I would have snapping on his ass too." Tamika said.

"Yep, but it's good. He is doing him, so I'ma damn sure do me."

"I hear that girl." Anya said.

"Anyways. Are you excited to get out of this bullshit snow tomorrow?" Taji asked me.

"Hell yea." I said.

"Where are you going?" Anya asked.

"To Vegas." I responded.

"Oh ok. Who are you going with?"

"Some friends."

"Some good friends." Taji said.

"Shut up Taji." I said and then I pushed her.

"Well, have fun for me. Shoot I will be stuck here in this nasty weather. We are supposed to get a lot of snow tomorrow."

I looked out the large picture windows at all the snow we already had on the ground.

"We don't need no more snow. We already got a bunch." I said.

Anya said, "Girl you know this is Minne-Snowta."

"True, and on that note, I am going to have a ball for all of y'all." I said.

I got a text message from Laron asking me if I wanted to ride with him and Paris to the airport or meet them there. I text him back and told him that I was going to meet them there. I don't mind riding with people, but I prefer to ride in my own car that way I can separate myself when I need to. I text message my sister to see what she was up to. She had been a little quiet, and I was sure because she was letting that lame ass dude Jamir bring her down again. She didn't text me back right away, so I put my phone away and turned my attention to the mirror as Tamika was putting the finishing touches on my hair weave.

"Oh, I love it." I said.

"Do you?"

"Yes."

"Good because it looks good on you." She smiled at me. I paid her and Taji and I left.

Chapter 7

Paris

It felt good to be in some warm weather after leaving a blizzard in Minnesota. I was enjoying the ninety-degree temperatures in Las Vegas, Nevada. It made me miss California. I thought about asking my husband to move back to California with me. The only reason he wanted to move home was to be closer to his mom before she passed from cancer. We kind of just got stuck there after she died. We really don't have anything holding us there. He was an only child. He never knew his dad and he only has a few aunts and some close cousins left in Minnesota. They could come visit us in the Golden State. I decided that I was going to talk to him about it when we returned to Minnesota after our vacation. The photoshoot and fashion show went well. It was cool having my husband and Raelyn there. She seemed like she enjoyed watching me do my thing. Since work was done, I was ready to turn up, party, and enjoy Las Vegas to the fullest with my husband and our new lover.

My husband, Raelyn, and I walked down the Las Vegas strip taking in the sights of all the huge hotels and palm trees around us. It was early and there were still a lot of other people on the strip doing the same thing that we were doing. Raelyn and I were shopping for tourist trinkets. We were also shopping for bathing suits to wear to the pool party at our hotel. My husband was tagging along watching us shop and waiting patiently to pay for whatever we wanted.

"Look at this one." Raelyn said. She held a gold bathing suit up.

"Oooo that is cute." I said and then I picked up a different one.

"What do you think about this?" I asked her.

"I love it."

"I hope you two found the ones you want finally."

Her and I laughed and then I said, "Hush babe."

He smiled and looked through a rack that had men t-shirts on it.

"Look at these shorts." Raelyn said.

"I like these too."

"We should get matching pairs."

"Ok."

We searched through the racks and found our sizes and then we took the bathing suits and shorts to the register. Laron paid for everything and then we left and headed back to our hotel to change.

Raelyn's body was killer in her gold bikini, and her new thirty-inch wet and wavy weave set the whole thing off. She was standing in our hotel room looking like a Goddess. I could see why my husband chose her. At that point, I still wasn't into women, but I felt attracted to her. I blamed my attraction on the alcohol. We had already taken a few shots of Patron, and I was already ready to get the party started.

"Oh, my god Raelyn you look too sexy in this." I said when she walked out of the bathroom "You think so?" she asked.

"Yes. Turn around." I said. She turned in a circle.

"Damn." Laron said.

She giggled and said, "Thanks you guys. You look good in yours too Paris." she said looking at my hot pink bikini.

In my mind, the Patron shots made me walk over to her, wrap my arms around her, palm her plump ass, and kiss her. It was a peck on the lips, but I knew that husband would like to see me do it, so I stepped outside of my comfort zone for him again.

"Both of y'all look sexy as hell. I'm a lucky man." Laron said before walking over to where we were standing.

He kissed both of us and smacked both our butts. Raelyn and I slipped into our matching shorts, put on our heels, put on our shades, and grabbed towels.

"Babe take some pics of us." I said.

Raelyn and I posed while Laron took several pics of us with each of our phones, and then her and I took turns taking pics with him. After we were done with our mini photo shoot, the three of us left the hotel room and took the elevator down to the first floor to the pool party.

***

All three of us were highly intoxicated after the pool party. I remember stumbling a little bit and giggling on our way back to our hotel room. Our plan was to take a shower, get dressed, and head out to a club, but we ended up in bed for an intense love making session before making it out of the door. I remember that it started with me and Raelyn. We had both finished our shower and we were sitting on the edge of one of the hotel room beds wrapped in our white hotel towels. I went in for a kiss and it escalated from there. By the time Laron got out of the shower, I was kissing and sucking on her sacred center.

"Ah. I see you got things started for me wifey." my husband said when he walked up to the bed.

"Um hum." I hummed and then I turned to smile at him. Raelyn giggled in between moans.

"Shit, y'all look good. Don't stop. Let me see what that mouth do, wifey." he said.

My husband stood back and watched me taking sips of her sweet nectar until his manhood stiffened. I was making loud slurping sounds like I was sipping the best hot tea from out of a cup, or like I was eating a bowl of hot soup.

"Damn wifey you're doing that shit." he said as he stood at the foot of the bed with his swollen chocolate bar in his hand.

He told Raelyn and I to come to him and get a taste. Both of us crawled across the bed where my husband was standing and took his manhood into our mouths. We both took turns licking and sucking on him, and then we sucked him together. My husband watched as our tongues massaged him all the way up to the tip and then connected with each other's, and then we tongue kissed each other while tongue kissing the tip.

"Damn." he moaned while he watched us devour him like chocolate candy.

The look in his eyes told me that he was in heaven. I was happy to be giving my man and my husband the kind of pleasure that he wanted. He tilted his head back and closed his eyes and I knew that he was heading to the point of no return.

"Mmm, shit." my husband moaned, and then before he reached the point of explosion he told us to stop.

He said, "Taste each other."

We moved away from him and got into a sixty-nine position. Raelyn on top and me on the bottom. My husband held his erection in his hands as he kept his eyes on me licking Raelyn, and Raelyn sucking on me. He walked from one side of the bed to the other to get a view of both ends of the sixty-nine, and then he walked back to my end. He entered Raelyn doggy style while she was still on top of me in a sixty-nine position. I watched as my husband began pumping in and out of Raelyn while I continued to taste her. I took my tongue off her for a second to taste his jewels and then I put it back on her. She started moaning from the feeling of being penetrated and licked at the same time. I was moaning from the feeling of her tongue on my peach. He was moaning from the feeling of being inside her.

"You like that baby?" he asked Raelyn.

She moaned, "Yes."

"That's right wifey, stay on her." he said to me. I kept my tongue flicking her pearl. She continued licking and sucking on mine. I continued to watch my husband go in and out of her until she reached her orgasm. She stopped licking me and let out sounds of pleasure mixed with a few curse words.

"Shit!" she yelled.

"That's it baby." Laron said to her.

She whined and moaned some more as she got hers. My husband pulled out of her and told her to lay on her back. He told me to sit it on her tongue and face him. I crawled to her and kissed her first before putting my sweet center on her mouth. I grinded my hips on her tongue and stared into my husband's eyes while he pounded into her wetness. I rubbed my nipples and grinded. He watched and pounded.

"That's right wifey."

"This is so sexy." I said.

"Um hum." he moaned.

He stayed in her and I kept grinding until I had an intense orgasm.

Ahh! Oh my God!" I cried out.

Raelyn continued licking and tasting my juices while I shook and shivered. I climbed off her and laid on the side of them. I watched my husband make love to her the same way he did to me, and it didn't bother me. It turned me on even more. I slid up to her and began kissing her and then I climbed on top of her. He pulled out of her and put it in from the back. I arched my back while kissing her. I held still while he was giving me some aggressive thrusts.

"Mmmm. Yes. Baby." I moaned in between me and Raelyn kissing.

I told her to slide up so I could taste her again. She slid upwards until her peach was back at my face. I gave her my tongue while my husband gave me deep thrusts. We made sounds and we gave each other pleasure until my husband pulled out and busted on my ass.

"Uh! Shit!" he moaned out loud before releasing himself on me.

He stepped back still holding himself, and said, "Y'all sexy as hell."

We started giggling which made him chuckle a little as he wiped sweat from his forehead. He walked into the bathroom and came back with wet towels. After we cleaned ourselves, each one of us took another shower and got dressed to go out to a nightclub. Raelyn and I talked and laughed about how good sex with the three of us was while my husband was in the shower. Once we were all dressed, we headed out for the night. I am sure my husband had the time of his life in Vegas, and I was happy that I gave him what he wanted. I felt like we'd fallen deeper in love than we were before the sexual experience with Raelyn. In my mind, Priscilla was wrong about her theory. The threesome made our relationship better, so I thought.

Chapter 8

Raelyn

"How was Vegas?" Riley asked.

"It was nice." I responded. I winced from the burning feeling in my legs as I lifted the weight we had the machine set to. I was on set number three and I felt like my legs were going to give out on me.

"Did you do a bunch a freaky stuff with them?"

"Yes, and I loved it."

"You're nasty sister."

"I know, but you like me this way. You wanted me out of the shell, so now I am out."

"Yea you're are way out of that shell."

"Shut up." I said and laughed.

"I didn't tell you to mess with a couple sister."

"Well, I'm exploring my options."

"I mean, do you think it's going to go anywhere? How are you going to introduce them to mom and dad? As your future husband and wife? They would have a fit."

I laughed so hard that I lost control of the weights. I dropped them, and they made a loud clanging sound throughout the gym.

"Oh, my goodness Riley stop. I wasn't thinking that far into it." I said as I stood up.

She sat down and said, "I'm serious. This can't be a permanent situation for you sister. How long do you plan to be their play toy?"

"Play toy?"

"Yes. What else do you think you are to them?" There isn't a future in that. They are already married. It's not like he can marry you."

"Like I said, I haven't thought about that. I am just having fun."

"I'm saying sister, have your fun, but don't get too deep."

"I guess you have a point, and like I said for the third time, I wasn't thinking that far into it."

"You should."

"Well, they are coming to the club tonight, so you will get to meet them. I'm going to their house after work."

"For more freaky favors for them?"

"Anyways. What's up with the Jamir situation? I asked.

Riley replied, "I don't know."

"Are you messing with him again sister?"

"Yes."

"Why?"

"Because he makes me feel good."

"Yea, but only temporarily, and then when it's over, he is back to treating you like you're nothing. Didn't you just get done preaching to me about temporary situations?"

"It's different with him. He is not temporary. Me and Jamir are going to be together. He's been better this time.

"This time. Ok sister."

"I know that he loves me. He's just afraid to show it."

"Are you sure?" I asked. I followed her to a set of matching leg machines. Both of us sat down and set our weight, and then we began squeezing our legs together to work out our inner thighs muscles.

"Yes, I am sure. I can feel it."

"Ok sister. You're going to continue to let him toy around with your feelings.

"He's not. I want to introduce him to mom and dad."

I frowned. "Are you crazy?"

"What?" she asked.

"Do you really think he is worthy of meeting our parents?" I asked.

"Yes, I do. I think he is the one sister. Sometimes people just need time to grow. He is everything I want in a husband. He is handsome, goal oriented, driven, a working man, independent, and good in bed." she said.

"Independent? Didn't you just tell me that he was living with his mama?"

"Yea, but he is in a transition after his divorce. It's only temporary."

"Like your relationship." I said.

"Whatever sister."

I sighed and let the weight down slowly.

"I'm going to tell you like you just told me. Stop trying to make a temporary situation permanent."

She cut her eyes at me, and then she said a curt, "Whatever."

***

I looked at myself in the bathroom mirror while brushing my wet and wavy hair weave into a pony tail. I was thinking about what my sister said at the gym the whole time, and then I heard my phone ringing in my living room. I walked into my living room and picked up my phone from the coffee table. I answered my phone before sitting down on my couch.

"Hey Laron." I said.

"Hey baby. How are you?"

"I am doing good baby. Are you back in town?"

"Yea I just got back." he said.

"Kind of sucks that you had to leave right after Vegas."

"I know. I had to get to a job. I can't miss out on no money. Especially when I need to take care of my women. Y'all tried to break me in Vegas."

I laughed.

Laron said, "You know what?"

"What?"

"I haven't stopped thinking about you since Vegas. Shit, since we did what we did period. I didn't say anything because I didn't want you to feel uncomfortable."

"Oh." I giggled. "So, you liked it."

"Hell yea. I loved it. You know that I did. You and my wife look sexy as hell together, but you alone? Oh my God. I wasn't expecting you to have a little freak in you."

I laughed.

"Seriously, you definitely open up behind closed doors."

"You should see my toy closet and porn collection." I said and then I giggled.

"Oh yea? You got a toy closet?"

I laughed and said, "Yea. That is what I had going on before I met you."

"Wow. You a trip."

I laughed again.

"What are you doing right now?"

"Relaxing."

"I'm going to stop by to see you. I'm close by."

"Alright."

"I'll be there in five minutes."

I put my phone down and turned my attention to the television. I was in the middle of binge watching all six seasons of Scandal. I heard that the next season was going to be the last season, so I wanted to catch up. The Olivia Pope character was just getting it in with the character known as The President when my doorbell rang.

"Damn." I said as I stood up and walked to my door to buzz Laron into my apartment building. I continued to watch the television while I waited by the door for him to get there. I heard a knock at my door and opened it.

Laron smiled and said, "Hey baby."

I replied, "Hey."

He gently wrapped his arms around my waist and squeezed me in a tight hug. The skin from his arms rubbing against mine immediately aroused me. It sent a sensation to my love button. He was looking good and smelling delicious as usual.

"I missed you." he said and then he kissed me.

"I missed you too." I responded after the kiss. He released his embrace and I closed and locked my door. He followed me to the couch.

"It's been a while since I've been alone with you." he said after sitting down.

"I know. Well, it hasn't been that long." I said and then I sat down.

"Long enough." Laron said and then he pulled me into his arms.

I laid my head on his chest and curled my legs up on the couch. Both of our attention was on the television for a little while and then our lips found each other's. Our lip locking lasted longer than usual. It was a long kiss that felt like it would never stop, and I didn't think either of us wanted to stop. Laron's hands began to wonder again, and then he caught himself again.

"Let me chill." he said.

"I'm sorry." I said.

"No. Don't be baby. I love you and I love being around you, but it's hard to be around you and not want you."

"I understand. I feel the same and I love you too."

"Oh, you want me too?" he asked.

I giggled and said, "Of course, I do."

"I don't want you to think that this is just a sexual thing. I really have feelings for you."

"Does Paris know that?"

"She does. I told her."

"And she is ok with that?"

"She is chill, and she is cool with it. She likes you too, so she has given me the green light on you, but she wouldn't let this shit fly with nobody else."

"To be honest, I wouldn't let that shit fly with nobody." I said.

"When you're in love with somebody, you would be surprised what you would be willing to do. You stepped outside of your box for me too."

"I guess you have a point." I said and then our lips found each other's again. I could feel my love button thumping like a heartbeat.

"I want to see your closet." he said in between kisses.

"Huh?" I asked.

"Your toy, closet. I want to see it." he replied through kisses.

"Really?" I asked.

"Um hum. Take me to it."

I sucked his bottom lip and then I stood up and put my hand in his. He stood up and followed me to my bedroom. I walked over to my armoire and opened the double doors. There were toys lined up in every color, size, and shape.

Laron's eyebrows went up. "Damn."

I laughed and said, "I know. It's kind of embarrassing."

"No, it adds to your sexiness."

"This was my life before you came in it."

"You got some shit in here. What does this purple one do?"

"It's a dual pleasure. It vibrates and twists inside me and the two rabbit ears give my clit pleasure."

He picked it up and turned it on. It started moving around. He laughed and said, "I've never seen no shit like this before."

"Paris doesn't have toys?"

"No. She would never mess with this kind of stuff. She is open sexually, but not on this level. She tries new things with me like the threesome with you, or going to sex parties, but this is over and beyond for her.

"Y'all been to sex parties?"

"Um hum. Once or twice, but we never did anything there. We just watched."

"Now that, is over and beyond for me."

"We could take you sometime. If you want to go."

"I don't know if I am ready for that."

He laughed and turned the toy off. "I want to see."

"See what?"

"You play with this."

"Seriously?"

"Um hum."

"I've never done it in front of anybody."

"Well let me be the first one."

I thought about it for a second and then I smiled and took the toy from him.

"Get naked. I want to see all of you."

I took all my clothes off and laid on the bed. I turned the toy on and then I inserted it into my box. I began moaning when I felt the vibration inside of my wet center and the little rabbit ears working my love button. Laron stood there and watched the toy disappear and reappear. I pushed it in and out of me slowly just like I like it.

"Hmm. Damn girl. You look sexy as hell." he said. He bit his bottom lip and grabbed the crotch of his jeans.

He reached into the closet and grabbed a sliver one that didn't have the rabbit ears.

"What does this do?"

"It's a vibrator."

"Can I try this?"

"Yea."

He took his shoes off and kneeled in front of me. He turned the silver vibrator on and put it inside of me. He pushed the sleek silver machine in and out of me. I started making sounds of pleasure as I put my hands on my breasts and started gently squeezing my nipples.

"Shit, girl, you are sexy." he said.

"Mmm." I moaned.

"Can I taste it?" he asked.

I moaned, "Yes."

Laron kept the silver vibrator inside of me as he put his mouth on me and started flicking his tongue on my pearl.

"Oh myyyy…." I moaned. I couldn't get my whole sentence out it felt so good. I wound my hips against the silver vibrator and his tongue.

"Cum for me" Laron whispered. He kept working his tongue on my pearl until I froze from my orgasm.

"Ah baby!" I hollered out.

Laron pulled the vibrator out and watched me lose it. He turned it off and set it on the bed next to me. He climbed on top of me and started kissing me.

He whispered, "I want to feel you again."

"I'm gonna be with y'all tonight." I responded.

"I'm talking about right now." he whispered while removing his jeans.

"What about Paris?"

"She doesn't care. She knows. I told her that I was coming here."

"Not to have sex."

"Trust me. She is aware."

He already had his boxers off and his manhood in his hand. He put himself inside me before I could say another word or ask another question, and then he whispered, "I want to see those faces you made in Vegas."

I didn't give it another thought. I wanted to feel him inside me just as bad as he wanted to be inside me. Their arrangement was their arrangement. I had nothing to do with that. I wrapped my legs around him and let him have all of me.

That was the first time that we were making love to each other without Paris. Our first time making love to just each other, and it felt way better than being with him and his wife. He was giving me so much energy. I felt like I wanted to scream it felt so good. As he was grinding his thickness into me slowly, I felt his tongue on my neck. He was twirling circles on my neck, and then he gently slid his tongue up to my earlobe. He sucked and nibbled on my earlobe before dipping his tongue into my ear. He had my box feeling like a lake. I squinted my eyes and let my head tilt back. My mouth fell half way open as I entered orgasm heaven. He stayed on my G spot and kept his tongue in my ear until my walls tightened around him. I exploded onto his manhood, and I moaned a few obscenities before mentally returning to earth.

"Shit Laron!" I said.

I opened my eyes and watched Laron pull out of me. He kissed my body back down to my pearl and gently sucked on it until I begged him to stop.

"Baby pleaaaasee. I can't take it." I moaned.

I scooted back, and he smiled and pulled me back to him. He continued to lick on my love button until I screamed, "Ahhh! Baby! Fuck!"

He stopped and let my body tremble. He had a grin of satisfaction on his face while watching me lose it again.

After I came back down from another orgasm, I slid backwards, got on my knees, and then crawled to him. I wanted to taste him. I had wanted to taste him since before news of his wife. I wanted to give him what he had given me many times. I put his manhood in my mouth and sucked my juices off him. He moaned and had a look of shock on his face when he felt me take every inch of him into my mouth. I hadn't done that while having sex with him and his wife because I didn't want to show her up. I didn't want to do too much and make her feel uncomfortable with me being there. She wasn't there, so I could do everything I had wanted to do to Laron without holding back. I used a lot of saliva while sliding my mouth, lips, and tongue up and down his shaft slowly. I took him out of my mouth just to massage it with my hand while I dropped a little saliva on it. I dropped a little more saliva on it and looked up at him while massaging it.

"Damn. Suck that dick girl." he said.

I let go of it and put him back into my mouth with no hands. I sucked my saliva off him and sped up the pace. I sucked him with no hands while looking up at him. I slurped and sucked on him like a popsicle that was on the verge of melting under the hot sun. I sucked him like I was trying to stop the juice from a watermelon from dripping down my chin. I slurped and sucked on him like it was the last few licks I had on a lollipop before I could get to the bubble gum center. I had so much saliva on him that it was dripping off my lips and onto the bed.

"Daaaamn Raelyn. Shiit." he moaned.

Laron watched me in awe of my work on his chocolate bar. He stood frozen watching me until he couldn't take it anymore, and then he started begging me to stop.

"Oooo shit baby you're about to make me cum. Baby wait. I don't want to cum yet."

I kept going until I felt him swell up in my mouth, and right when I knew he was on the edge I stopped. His mouth flew open and he grabbed himself like he couldn't believe what I had just done, and then he quickly bent me over and dove inside me. He started banging my peach intensely. He put his hands on my ass and smacked it every few seconds. I bounced my ass back on him like a stripper, or a porn star. I was twerking my thing better than one of those chicks in those twerk videos on YouTube. He smacked my ass again, so I looked back at him and told him not to stop.

"Don't stop baby. I like that." I said.

He grunted and lost himself.

"Ahhhhhh!" he groaned and then he pulled out of me and squirted so hard it landed in my hair.

"Shiiit!" he yelled out as he was holding himself. As he was trying to catch his breath, I turned around and sucked the rest of his nut out of him until he went soft.

He said, "Raelyn. Damn. You a certified freak." In between breaths.

I laughed and backed up off him. I climbed out of the bed to get us some towels. I came back wiping his nut out of my hair. I handed him a towel.

"Naw for real." he said. "You know damn well you were holding back during the threesome."

I giggled. "I was."

He chuckled. "I am sorry about your hair baby."

"It's ok I can wash it."

"That shit was too good girl. I couldn't control it."

"I'm not done."

"Oh, you want some more?"

"Um hum. Don't you?" I asked with a seductive grin.

"Hell yea. Give me five minutes and I got you."

Chapter 9

Riley

"You should let me record you doing that shit boo." Jamir said to Riley. He was looking down at her while she was on her knees giving him head. She had ambushed him while he was in the bathroom washing his hands for the dinner she'd cooked for him.

Riley stopped and giggled.

"For real boo, I want to show you how sexy you look."

"Ok babe, only for you. You better not show anyone."

"That's what I'm talking about. That's why you're my boo. This is for me and your eyes only."

He pulled his phone out and pressed record. Riley put on a show for the camera. Slurping and deep throating all of him. She had practiced and learned how to relax her jaws and throat so she could take all of him into her mouth. She was determined to show him that she was the woman for him in every way possible.

"That's right baby. Look at that shit. No hands. You a pro with it. Look up at me." Jamir said.

Riley looked up at the camera with the sexiest lustful look she could give while slurping and sucking on Jamir until he busted into her mouth. Riley swallowed every drop, and then she stuck her tongue out to the camera and smiled.

Jamir laughed and said, "You're nasty girl."

***

Riley rolled out of bed early the next day to get cleaned up and make breakfast for her boo Jamir. It had been a while since he'd spent the night at her house. She wanted to surprise him with breakfast in bed. Riley took a bath and put on a pair of short shorts and a tank top. She smiled at the fine, ebony, hunk of man lying in her bed sleeping as she made her way to the kitchen. She turned on the stove and spent the next thirty minutes hooking up some pancakes, eggs, grits, and bacon. When she finished, she carried the plate of food to her bedroom. Riley nudged Jamir a few times to wake him up. Jamir woke up and smiled when he saw Riley standing there with a plate of steaming food. "You did all this?"

"Yes. It's been a while since I've cooked for you."

"Thank you." he said. Jamir took the plate of food from her and set the plate of food on the night stand.

"I could do it more often, if you stayed over more." Riley said.

Jamir pulled Riley into the bed by her arm. He wrapped her up into his arms and kissed her on the forehead.

"You gonna stop talking shit you hear me?"

Riley laughed and said, "I'm just saying."

"Yea, yea. Whatever."

Jamir sat up and got out of the bed. He went to the bathroom to clean himself up. Jamir had a tooth brush and some his man products in Riley's bathroom. He even had some clothes in her closet the he'd left over there for the times he stayed the whole night. Jamir got back into the bed and kissed Riley and pulled her close to him. He picked up his plate of food and began eating. Riley found much joy in watching him eat her cooking.

"This shit good boo." Jamir said between chews. He gave her a kiss after swallowing a few bites. Riley smiled at him and then slid away from him to go into the kitchen.

"Where are you going?" he asked as he set the plate back on the nightstand.

"To get something to drink."

"Nah, you staying right here."

Jamir pulled Riley back into the bed and then he climbed on top of her. She gave him a seductive smile, opened her legs, and wrapped them around him.

He said, "I'm about to put this D in you."

Riley giggled.

"You want it, don't you?" Jamir said as he pulled her shorts off.

"Um hum." Riley smiled. He touched her box to see how wet it was. When he felt her juices, he smiled and said, "I knew you wanted it.

He put his finger in her mouth and watched her suck her juices off it and then he slid his tool inside of her. Riley loved when Jamir would stay all night, so he could give her that good morning sex that she loves.

Jamir put her legs onto his shoulder and dug deep into Riley. He stayed deep in it until she started to sing tunes, saying his name, and calling for God. When Riley reached her O, Jamir kept going until he felt her legs start to tremble. He took her legs off his shoulder and spread them apart. He deep stroked her in that position until she came again and started to run from him.

"Ahh fuck." she said as she tried to push him away and move backwards.

"Uh, uh. Where you going? What I tell you about running from me. You better take this dick." Jamir said.

He snatched Riley back to him by her legs

"Ahh Jamir." she cried out.

"That's right. Whose pussy is this?"

"Mmmm. It's yours." Riley moaned.

"Uh, huh, and it always will be."

"I love you Jamir."

"I know you do. Do you love this dick?"

"Yes, baby I do."

"You better."

"Shit baby, right there."

"Um hum. Right there what?"

"Right. There. Baby. I'm about to cum." Riley said.

Jamir felt her juices pour down on him like heavy rain. He looked down at all her juices all over his manhood and then he looked back up at her.

"Damn boo." he said and then he smiled.

Jamir watched Riley's body shake and shiver from her orgasm, and then he pounded even harder into her. Riley's peach made sounds from him plunging into her wetness. Jamir kept her right on the edge of tapping out for a few more minutes and then he pulled out. He stepped back and watched her curl up into a fetal position. Jamir was proud that he'd put it down again and left Riley speechless.

Chapter 10

Raelyn

I poured some white wine into a glass and then I handed it to my customer. They handed me some cash and told me to keep the change. They walked off into the night club. I waited for Riley to finish making the Long Island Iced Tea for her customer. It was a slow night at the club. It was winter season, and people weren't out as much. Riley walked over to me after her customer walked away and we chatted for a while. We saw Laron and Paris walk into the nightclub holding hands.

"Isn't that your boo and his wife?"

"Yep." I smiled and walked to the front of the bar to greet them.

"Hey!" Paris said.

"Hi!" I responded. I leaned over the bar to give them both a hug.

"Hey baby." Laron said to me. He gave me a hug and a kiss on the cheek.

"Ready to hang when you get off work?" he asked.

"Hell yes." I smiled.

"Oh my gosh, is this your sister?" Paris exclaimed.

"Yes. Riley this is Paris and Laron."

"Hello. Nice to meet you both."

Paris said, "You two are identical. Wow."

Riley and I giggled like we always do every time someone is shocked about us being twins.

"I've got to go. You guys have a good-time."

Riley walked over to another customer to take their drink order.

I said, "I'm going to make your drinks."

I walked away and made their drinks on the house. After I gave them the drinks I made, Riley and I stood back and watched them walk to the dance floor. Since it was a slow night, the DJ didn't have the music volume pumped up to the max as usual, but he was still playing all the hits. As they began dancing with each other, I smiled. They were a beautiful looking couple.

"Look at that. Do you see the looks in their eyes? They're in love."

I observed them some more, and for the first time since we'd all had sex, I felt like an outsider. *Maybe I'm just letting Riley get into my head. It's been more than just a sex thing with me and him. Furthermore, the way he made love to me earlier let me know that his feelings are involved. Riley does have a point. It's not like I can really be his woman. I am not the type to try to make a man leave the one he is with either.* I thought.

"Yea, but he loves me too sister."

"Sister, she loves that man too much. You ain't nothing but one of his little toys. I'm telling you." Riley said.

"She likes me though."

"No, she doesn't. She loves him."

Riley walked away to help the next customer.

***

Laron poured chocolate all over me and Paris's bodies. He watched us lick it off each other, and then he joined in. He feasted on us one by one. Laron started with me. He went straight for my box and began slurping left over chocolate from my lips, and then he put his tongue on my love button and went to work. He was licking and sucking on my pearl slow; savoring the taste of my essence while Paris was sucking on his manhood.

"Mmm." he moaned as he licked and sucked on me.

I moaned in return as I watched him dip his tongue in and out of me and then make his way back to my pearl. He focused on my love button and flicked his tongue rapidly on it, and then he sucked on it again.

He stopped and said, "Uh-uh. I don't want to make you cum. I want my wife to make you cum." Laron stopped tasting me and told Paris to lay down next to me so he could taste her.

Laron looked at me and said, "Sit on her face."

"Mmm baby." she moaned as he buried his lips and face into her lotus blossom. I crawled over and put it on her face. The feeling of her soft tongue on me sent me into another world as it always. She was always way gentler than Laron. The tip of her tongue felt like a feather on my pearl. I looked down at her as I felt my orgasm nearing.

"Ah! Shit!" I moaned loudly.

"That's right wifey. She tastes good, don't she?" Laron said in between licks.

"Um hum." Paris moaned from under me.

I climbed off her and laid next to them to catch my breath for a second. Laron laid down and told her to get on top of him. As I watched her riding him, I noticed that same look of love in her eyes that my sister and I saw at the club. The way she looked at him never mattered to me before my sister mentioned it, but suddenly it was noticeable. I ignored it and got back into the moment. I crawled over to Paris and sucked on her nipples. She moaned and rubbed her fingers through my flat ironed hair. Laron told me to come to him. I climbed on top of him and faced her. We moaned together and watched each other getting what we wanted. She got hers and stopped moving. She collapsed next to him while catching her breath. I got mine and laid down next to him. He kissed her and then he climbed on top of me. She watched him make love to me. The look in her eyes made me question whether she was enjoying it still. Maybe it was the way he was gazing into my eyes while he was giving me the business. I could tell that her mind drifted for a second just like mine had and then she got back into the moment.

Paris crawled over to me and began kissing me seductively while looking at him. That's when I realized that it was all for him. The bond that her and I created wasn't because she liked me. It was because she wanted to please her husband and because she would do anything for him. Maybe Laron was doing it just to please himself. I started to feel like I *was* their toy just like my sister said. I stayed in the moment. I didn't want to kill the vibe, but I knew that when I got home, I was going to rethink the whole situation with them. My feelings had gotten way too involved with Laron.

Maybe now that I am open to dating again, it's time to find someone of my own. I can't be in love with someone else's husband. Even if the sex is good. I thought.

Chapter 11

Raelyn

A week and a half later, Riley and I were walking out of the club we work at with Taji at the end of our work night. Taji had gone out with some of her other friends and decided to hang around after the club closed so she could go to breakfast with us. That was when all hell broke loose. We walked out of the front door instead of the back like we usually do because Taji wanted to walk through the club let out scene. Most of the time, the club let out is everyone that was in the club standing around outside having drunk conversation. Sometimes people who didn't even go to the club show up for club let out just to see who is out and about or hoping for some action to pop off.

There was snow on the ground, but it wasn't that cold outside. Riley and I had on our waist length North Face coats with UGG boots and Taji was rocking a leather coat with a pair of expensive looking, knee-high, stiletto heeled boots. We were walking through the crowd of people, when Taji spotted her dude standing on the corner talking to the stripper chick from Instagram she had told me about at the salon. I don't know why he was out there with that girl or how they got out there together, but Taji lost her mind. She stormed straight over to them.

"What the fuck are you doing down here with this bitch!?" Taji yelled. Riley and I stopped walking.

"Aye! What the hell!" Her man yelled. He put his arm in front her to block her from getting any closer.

"Who are you calling a bitch!" the girl said.

"You, bitch!" Taji yelled.

Taji's man stepped in between them and spoke to the stripper. "I'll holla at you later."

"You better get your bitch!" the girl yelled.

Taji reached for the girl, but her man stopped her. "Stop!" he yelled as he grabbed Taji's arm and pulled her away from the girl.

"Bitch!" Taji called back at the girl.

Riley and I stood there with our eyebrows raised watching the whole scene. Some people gathered around to watch with us.

"What the fuck is your problem!? Why are you down here wilding out and shit!" he yelled at Taji as he continued to pull her down the block towards his car.

"Why are you down here with her!?" Taji yelled back.

"I wasn't down here with her!"

"So, I'm blind!?"

"Hell no! Get in the car Taji!" he said as he opened the car door. He still had her arm in his hand.

"Let me go!" He let go of her arm. She got in his car and he slammed the door. He got in the driver's side and they sped off down the street.

"Damn his bitch buck." some guy said. A few people started laughing and then Riley and I started laughing.

"What the hell was that sister?" Riley asked me.

"I don't know. A damn circus act." I said through laughs as we walked towards our cars.

"I just felt like we were on the set of Jerry Springer."

"I know right." I said.

"Taji and her man never fail to entertain."

"I know. I guess she is not coming to breakfast."

"Nope." Riley said.

I laughed, and when we hit the corner, we ran into Jamir and a group of people coming out of the pizza spot. My eyes went straight to all the females that were in the group. They were all dressed in next to nothing in the winter. It wasn't that cold, but it wasn't warm enough for what they had on. First Taji, and then Jamir. That night couldn't have gotten any better. I noticed that Jamir's body language was off. He didn't seem happy to see Riley down there.

"What's up?" he asked when he approached Riley.

Jamir was rocking a knit University of Minnesota hat and a brown leather coat. He was looking at Riley with those sexy, deep brown, bedroom eyes that I knew she was hooked on.

"Hey. What are you doing down here? I thought you said that you were at home tonight."

"Yea. I'm out with my boys. It was last minute."

"And them?" Riley asked speaking of the women he was with.

"Oh, they are with my boys. They ain't got shit to do with me."

"Hmmm. Ok."

"I got to go. I will hit you up later."

"Alright." she responded. I could tell that she was irritated.

He looked at me and said, "Alright Raelyn. Good seeing you."

I gave him a half smile and a half of a wave and then I turned my attention back to my sister. I noticed the he didn't hug or kiss my sister. He treated her like she was his homegirl. Laron hugged and kissed me all the time in public and he was married. Something wasn't right with Jamir and I knew it from the start. I wanted my sister to leave his no-good ass alone. Jamir was fine as hell, but Riley could do better than him. I felt that she had to know that. I felt that there was no way that my sister was that sprung, but I guess I was wrong.

I said, "Sister, I know, that you know, that he was lying."

"He has no reason to."

"Come on now. There were four chicks and four guys, and not one of those women were for him?"

"That's what he says. I have no reason to not believe him."

"Come on Riley. You can't be that blind. Did you see his body language? Look, I've been told that he is a hoe and I saw him with another chick before."

Riley copped an attitude and said, "And your just now telling me?"

"I didn't want to kill your joy, but I can't sit and watch you get played."

"Look, why are you judging my situation?"

"I'm not. I'm just trying to protect you from getting your heart broke."

"Says the chick that is fucking a couple."

"Really Riley? I can't believe that you think that this dude is into you like that."

"And I can't believe you think that fucking a bitch and her man is ok. That dude doesn't want *you,* but am I all in your business? No. So, stay the fuck out of mine."

"Fuck you Riley." I started walking towards my car.

"No. Fuck you Raelyn. Keep fucking your man and his bitch!" she called after me.

"Keep fucking a nigga who got somebody else and don't want you!" I yelled down the alley at her. I slammed my car door. She slammed hers and sped off before me. After all that drama, we were no longer doing breakfast. I went home.

Chapter 12

Riley

Since Riley wasn't talking to her sister, she called their friend Cherry to get together for some food and girl chat. She hadn't seen her in a while and she was not in the mood for Taji and her man's drama. Cherry is laid back and her personality matches Riley's a little more than Taji's does. Riley and Cherry met at Barrio downtown Minneapolis for lunch. Cherry was already there when Riley walked in. Cherry stood up and hugged Riley when she approached the table.

"Girl why do you got me in this tiny boutique looking place? You know I'm a thick girl. I need some room." Cherry said.

Riley laughed and sat down in the stool seat on one side of the table. Cherry sat back down in the booth style seat on the other side of the table.

"So, fill me in on the latest drama." Cherry said and then she took a sip from her water.

"Oh my gosh. You have missed so much."

"I know I have. You know I stay under the radar. I don't come out much, but when I do, you always have something to tell."

Riley laughed and said, "Well, for starters, Taji and her boyfriend."

Cherry rolled her eyes and said, "Girl, stop. I can't with them."

"Girl they have gotten worse." Riley said.

"See that is the reason that I don't hang out with Taji much. Because I ain't got time for her and her dudes mess. I got my own stuff to deal with."

"Me either. She hangs with my sister a lot."

"I don't know how your sister does it."

"I don't either." Riley laughed.

"Honestly, if she dropped that dude I could kick it with her. She needs to stop letting that dude dim her light and push on with her modeling career. She is too busy chasing him around to focus."

"Yea."

They stopped talking for a minute to order margarita's and appetizers from the waiter.

Cherry asked, "So, what happened?"

"Taji spotted her dude downtown with another girl and went ham."

"Nah, she didn't go hard as a mutha fucka."

"Yes."

"Oh no. It was a huge scene, huh?"

"Yes, me and Raelyn were just watching."

Cherry laughed. "Wow. That is not the first time she has spotted him with another chick."

Riley laughed. "I know. That is not the half."

"Oh boy."

"After they leave, I see my dude with a bunch of people coming out of the pizza spot."

"Pizza Luce?"

"Yup."

"Some chicks?"

"Yes."

"Uh-uh."

They paused the conversation, so the waiter could put their food and drinks on table.

"Look at these little ass plates." Cherry said after the waiter walked away. She looked at Riley and said, "Next time we are going to Famous Dave's. I ain't no little tweety bird like you and your sister. I need some food."

Riley laughed and took a sip of her drink.

"Anyways. Jamir was acting all funny."

"Probably because he was with them chicks."

"Well, that's what Rae said and then me and her got into it."

"What?"

"Yep."

"You and your sister?"

"Yep and we haven't talked in a few weeks."

"Y'all rarely argue. Y'all need to stop."

"I know. I can't even tell her that I was pregnant by Jamir and I had a miscarriage."

"What!?"

"Yea."

"Does he know?"

"No."

"Now I know that you don't want to hear it, but you know that dude isn't any good Ri."

"He's a good dude. I think he is just scared to commit to someone because he just got out of a marriage. I'm sure he has some trust issues and some more stuff, but he just needs to see that I am not going to hurt him, and everything will be ok."

"Ri."

"What?"

"If that is what you think then the only thing I can tell you is do you, but there are plenty of other men out here then to be holding on to one who isn't treating you like the queen you are."

"I hear you."

"I think that is all your sister was probably expressing to you. I am sure that it didn't come out right because she is your sister. She is your twin at that and she can feel your pain."

Riley nodded her head.

"You should talk to her." Cherry said.

"I will."

Chapter 13

Raelyn

I was sitting next to Laron on the couch at his house. We were waiting for Paris to put her shoes and coat on so we could leave and then Laron whispered in my ear.

"You know that I love how your pussy tastes."

He stuck his tongue in my ear and I pushed him away and started giggling, and then he started laughing. Paris walked into the living room ready to go.

She asked, "What are y'all laughing at?"

"Nothing baby. I just told Raelyn that her shoes look like elf's."

She looked at us funny and then she looked down at my shoes.

"Yea boo those shoes."

I played along and started laughing. "Look y'all are going to get up off my shoes. These are high fashion."

They started laughing with me, but that was the first time I'd heard Laron lie to Paris. I made a mental note of it and kept it smooth.

"You look gorgeous as usual Paris."

"Thanks. You do too." she responded.

"Are you too ready to go?" Laron asked. He stood up and then he helped me stand up. The three of us headed out the door to go to a comedy show.

***

It might have been me, but it seemed like Paris was holding her husband a little closer than usual that night, but maybe I was holding him a little closer than usual and perhaps it was noticeable. I didn't feel like me or Laron had changed since our sexual encounter with each other, but possibly we had and didn't realize it. It had been months since the three of us had sex the first time, and he and I were spending a lot of time together. I started to question whether Paris was aware of how deep in love Laron and I had fallen for each other. Then, I told myself that she had to know because he told me that they talked about it and that she was comfortable with it. There was no way that she could've felt threatened by me because we were all in it together. Then, I thought about what my sister said about being their play toy and about fucking a chick and her man. I started going through the motions in my head again. *Riley might have had a point. Laron is not mine. He can't ever be mine. Why would I allow myself to fall in love with another woman's husband?* I thought.

"Baby are you ok?" Laron whispered to me.

"Yes." I whispered back.

He kissed my forehead and put his hand into mine. I looked over and saw Paris with her arm wrapped around his cracking up at whatever the comedian was saying. She looked over and smiled at me. I smiled back and realized that I had been so wrapped up in my thoughts that I didn't hear anything the comedian had said. I hadn't laughed once. Suddenly the sound of the large crowd around us laughing became clear and I realized I was the only one not laughing. That was probably why Laron asked if I was alright. I turned my attention back to the comedian on stage and caught the last joke. All three of us started cracking up.

***

There you go wifey. I like that shit right there." Laron said. He had just pulled out of Paris and bent down to taste her plum center. I was riding her face while holding on to the headboard.

"Ahh!" I moaned and then she cried out, "Uhhh baby! Yes! I cuming!"

After she busted, Laron stood up and pushed his love inside of her. He pushed her legs wide open and started putting his pound game down hard on her. He had the headboard that I was holding knocking. I was still riding her face and she was sucking my flower like she was trying to get honey out of it. She was making all the loud slurping sounds that Laron loves.

"Ah! Baby!" Paris cried out again, and then I yelled, "Shit! I'm cuming."

"Uh huh. Get yours, baby." I let my water fall onto Paris's lips.

"Mmm." she said when she tasted my nectar.

"She tastes good don't she wifey." Laron said.

"Um hum" she hummed and then I crawled off her face. Laron leaned down and started kissing my juices off Paris's lips, and then he said that he was about to bust. He pulled out and let himself go on her stomach. He kissed her again and then he said, "Come here Rae."

I crawled to him and he kissed me. He got up and got us towels to clean up with and then he lay in between us as always and we passed out. Well they did. I was too trapped in my thoughts to get into a good sleep. I felt like an outsider, so I lay there for a few hours and then I got up. I gently removed Laron's arm from around me and got out of bed. I started getting dressed to leave. My plan was to creep out without them knowing, but Laron woke up.

"Hey baby. Are you leaving." he whispered.

"Yea I have to meet up with my sister earlier than usual today to go to the gym and then go to our parent's house." I whispered.

I lied. I still hadn't talked to my sister since our verbal altercation. I just wanted to get out of there.

Laron looked at the clock, and whispered, "It's four in the morning baby."

"I know. We are hooking up at six." I whispered back.

"Alright, well let me walk you to the door."

He quietly slid out of the bed and followed me down the stairs and to the front door.

"Call me when you get home baby ok?" he said.

"Ok."

"I love you." he said.

"I love you too."

***

I never went to my parent's house that day, but I did a few days later for my dad's birthday dinner. His birthday falls a few days before the new year. I wasn't excited to go because I didn't want to act happy to be around my sister when I wasn't. I had done enough of that at work. I was still mad at her for how she attacked me for caring about her. We avoided all conversation with each other at work, but we couldn't do that in front of our parents because they would start asking us a bunch of questions.

When I got there, many of our family members and people from our church were there. People were sitting around the living room talking and laughing with my dad. A few of my cousins were sitting in fold out chairs up against the wall. My mom had streamers, balloons, and a happy birthday banner decorating the walls. Our dad was looking good dressed in all black. He was wearing a fitted black button up, some black slacks, a pair of dress shoes, and some black frames on his eyes. My dad swears he could model for GQ magazine or something. I walked over to my father, hugged and kissed him and handed him a gift.

"Thank you beautiful." he said. I hugged a few family and church members as I made my way through the house. I found my mom in the kitchen. I hugged and kissed her.

"Hey sweet pea." she said as she finished preparing the food. She was talking with one of my aunts. I spoke to my aunt and then found an empty spot to sit near the door. I was hoping to slip out after we sung the birthday song so I wouldn't have to talk to my sister.

My brother walked in a couple of minutes after me. "What's up scrub?" he said to me and then he walked over to my dad.

"Happy birthday pop."

"Hey son. Thank you."

He handed our dad a gift bag, and walked over to our mom, and then back over to me. My brother is a spitting image of our dad. He is tall, has a deep brown complexion, and a muscular build. He even sports a goatee on his face and his hair cut in a fade with waves on the top like our dad.

"Where is scrub number two?" Eazy asked me.

"I don't know." I said.

"Oh, what y'all beefing?"

"No."

"Uh huh. Y'all always know where each other are."

"We are grown with our own lives we aren't always on each other's tails."

"Um hum. Ok."

Riley walked in right after he asked me where she was. She did the same thing we did when we walked in. She spoke to our dad first, gave him a gift, and then headed over to our mom, and then over to us.

"Sup scrub two." Eazy said.

"Shut up." she said to him, and then there was an awkward silence between me and her.

"Um hum. Y'all two better work that shit out before mom and pop pick up on it because I ain't trying to be here all night with them two preaching to us about family sticking together." Eazy said. He walked over to help our mom finish putting the food on the table.

Riley looked at me and said, "Hey Rae."

"Hi Ri."

"Look, I apologize for the way I acted that night. I was frustrated and I felt like you were talking down on me." she said.

"Ri, I was just trying to tell you that I don't like seeing someone hurt you. You are my sister and I love you."

"I love you too Rae, and I am tired of not talking to you."

"I'm tired of it too." I said.

She smiled and said, "Good because I missed you."

"I missed you too. Don't you ever go a whole month without talking to me again." I said.

We hugged each other.

We heard our brother say, Thank God." He was standing behind us. "Now let's go sang happy birthday.

All of us walked over to the table with everyone else. We stood by our mom and dad. "Baby isn't it good to have all our kids here at the same time?" our mom said.

"Yes, it is."

"When are y'all coming to church?"

We laughed.

Eazy said, "We will be there Sunday mom. Ain't that right twins?"

"Yes." we responded in unison.

"Alight! Let's sing happy birthday."

Everyone at the party sang happy birthday the original way, and then we sung it the Stevie Wonder way. Our dad blew out his candle's, we cheered for him, and then we ate food, and then we had cake and ice cream for dessert.

"Y'all ready for this New Year's Eve party on Saturday? It's about to be lit!" Eazy said excitedly.

"Yup! We already got our dresses and masquerade masks ready."

"It better not be no sleazy stuff like at the Halloween party."

Riley hit him and said, "Shut up. There is nothing sleazy about a sexy S.W.A.T costume."

"Y'all had on them little shorts. You know what I am talking about."

Me and Riley started laughing and then I said, "Whatever Eazy we are grown. We can wear what we want."

"Um hum. I'm going to tell mom and pop y'all out here dressed to work a street corner at my parties."

Riley said, "Be quiet Eazy. They saw the pictures and they said that we looked cute. Ha!"

Eazy said, "Yea whatever. I'll see y'all Saturday."

Chapter 14

Riley

Raelyn and Riley were standing in the mirror at Raelyn's house looking at their matching black, sparkly, mini dresses. The dresses were short sleeve with plunging necklines that bared a lot of cleavage. They were both applying their make-up, so they could leave and get to the club. Both twins were wearing their hair in long, jet-black, hair weaves with a part down the middle. The dresses fit their bodies perfectly, but the dresses were short and revealing, so they knew their brother Eazy was going to be in his feelings.

"You know Eazy is going to be pissed when he sees these dresses." Raelyn said.

"I know, and I don't care." Riley said.

Raelyn laughed and put cherry red lip gloss on her lips. She handed Riley the bottle of lip gloss after she was finished.

"I've got to tell you something." Riley said.

Raelyn rubbed her hands over the top her hair and then she asked, "What?"

"I had a miscarriage."

Raelyn paused and looked at her sister. "What!?" Raelyn's face frowned as she dropped her hands from her hair and put them on her hips.

"Don't look at me like that sister."

"How the hell did you end up pregnant sister? You're not using condoms with Jamir?" she asked.

"Not anymore."

"Girl. You trust him like that?"

"It wasn't intentional. I guess we just got comfortable." Riley said. Raelyn smacked her lips and closed her eyes. It took everything in her not to start spewing all the negative feelings and thoughts she had about Jamir out of her mouth.

She stood there with her eyes closed for a second and then she said, "I'm sorry that happened to you sister."

Raelyn pulled Riley into her arms and hugged her.

"Thank you." Riley said.

Raelyn looked directly into her eyes and said, "Be careful. For real."

"I am."

"How do you feel about the miscarriage?"

"I was kind of sad when it happened, but I am fine now."

"Yea. Well everything happens for a reason sister."

"You sound like mom." she said as she readjusted her dress.

I said, "I know I do, and it is true."

"I hear you."

Raelyn and Riley turned back to the mirror to check their looks. They both agreed that they looked smoking hot.

"We look good." Riley said.

"Yes, we do. Let's take some pictures so we can get out of here." Raelyn said.

***

The night club was decorated in disco balls, glittery streamers, along with black and gold decorations. There was a big Happy New Year banner hanging by the DJ booth. They had Happy New Year party favors everywhere. Hats, glasses, and necklaces were at the front door, so the person collecting money could give them out as people came in. All the staff were dressed up in all black suits and dresses. Eazy walked up to the twins dressed in a tailor-made suit.

"I hope y'all ready tonight. Y'all are about to get caked up. It's about to be lit in here for real."

"We are always ready." Raelyn said.

"What's up with these little ass dresses?" he asked.

Riley said, "Eazy don't start."

He gave them a side eye and walked away.

Raelyn and Riley started giggling. "He is mad." Raelyn said.

"I know." Riley said.

"Oh well." Raelyn said as they headed to the back.

"Yo!" Riley said when she walked into the backroom.

A few of the bouncers and staff members were back chilling waiting to start the night. Everyone said hi to the twins.

"Sup twins." Shawn said.

"Sup Shawn." Raelyn said. Riley spoke to him and then put her purse in a locker.

"Y'all look nice." Shawn said.

"Thanks so do you." Raelyn said. She had never seen him dressed up. He cleaned up well. He even had his hair cut in a fade instead of his usual one level cut. Riley looked at the both them and smiled.

Riley and Raelyn put their masquerade masks on and went to the bar to make sure that it was set up before the doors opened fifteen minutes later.

"Why don't you give him a chance?" Riley asked Raelyn.

"Who?"

"Shawn."

"Sister stop. You know that I am involved."

Riley smacked her lips. "Sister. I'm not even about to go there, so, anyways, Shawn is nice and he likes you."

"He is not my type Riley."

"Oook." Riley sang.

The club had a crowd from the start. People crowded inside dressed in their best new year's outfits. The twins were working the busy bar tirelessly, but people were tipping well so they didn't mind.

Laron and Paris showed up to the party later that night and then Jamir showed up with a couple of his friends. Riley was excited to see him, but Raelyn and Paris had disgusted looks on their faces as he spoke to Riley and then Laron.

At least he gave you a hug this time." Raelyn said after he walked further into the club.

"Sister."

"Alright, I will shut up."

Taji walked in shortly after Jamir with some guy they'd never seen. They were both dressed to the nines with masquerade masks on. Riley could see that her friend was nicely built underneath his suit, but she didn't understand why Taji would be at the party with him. Especially after she'd acted a plum ass fool a month back when she spotted him downtown with another chick. Riley looked at Raelyn with a confused look on her face.

"Who is that?" Riley said.

"I don't know. She told me a while ago that she was seeing someone else on the side. This might be him."

"Oh hell no. I hope she don't be with that drama tonight."

"Me too."

"Hey Twins!" she said.

"Hey!" They responded.

"This is my friend y'all!" Taji said after she and him removed their masks.

The twins spoke to him, but they were confused. As he was ordering drinks for him and Taji, Cherry walked up.

She hugged Taji and gave the twins a funny look behind her back. She was also questioning the new guy.

"Who is this?" she asked Taji.

"This is my friend."

"Ok friend. Well, hello." Cherry said before she spoke to the twins. After she got a drink, she headed further into the club. Taji and her friend walked away from the bar and found a spot to stand by the wall.

"We killing it tonight!" Eazy said to the twins and then he disappeared in the crowd.

They smiled and made a few more drinks and then Riley looked up and saw Taji's man lurking in the crowd in regular street clothes and no mask. She knew that is was going to be trouble. She hurried over to Raelyn and tapped her on the shoulder.

"Sister look." Riley said.

"Oh no." Raelyn said.

"Should I go over there?"

"No sis. Stay out of it."

Just then, Cherry walked back up.

"Isn't that Taji's man?" she asked.

"Yup." The twins said in unison.

Laron and Paris walked over to say that they were leaving. Riley heard them tell Raelyn that they had another party to attend but they would see her later. After Raelyn hugged them goodbye, Riley turned her attention back to Taji and her friend. They didn't even see Taji's man coming. Cherry, Raelyn, and Riley all stood back watching. They knew there was about to be some drama and they hadn't even counted down to the new year yet.

"I'm going over there to tell her that he is in here." Cherry said. She walked quickly through the crowd to Taji. The twins watched her tell Taji to get out of there. Taji nodded her head and waved at the twins, but it was too late, her man had found them.

"Shit." Riley said.

He stepped to Taji and yelled something to her that they couldn't make out over the loud music. They saw Taji yell back. Cherry scurried away and found her way back to the bar with the twins.

Cherry said, "He asked her was that the dude she's been cheating on him with, and she said it was her friend. I got out of there after that."

"Oh man." Riley said as they continued to watch the argument between Taji and her man.

The three of them couldn't make out what else was being said over the loud music, but they could see Taji's man was heated. It looked like Taji's friend tried to intervene and pull Taji away from her dude, but Taji's dude swung and punched her friend in the face, and just that fast they were fighting. They were going at it like two dudes in a prison yard. They had fallen up against the wall and then ended up in the middle of the dance floor. Taji's dude was throwing some hard hits at Taji's friend, but the friend was holding his own. He was giving Taji's dude the business. The crowd had parted and started scrambling to get away. Some of the women were screaming, and the DJ had turned the music off.

The twins heard a few glasses break from them being knocked out of people hands as people were trying to get away.

"Uh oh looks like somebody has had too much to drink." he said over the microphone.

All the bouncers and Eazy ran over to break up the fight. The bouncers pulled Taji's man out the back door and Taji and her friend went out the front door.

The twins and Cherry shook their heads as they watched the whole scene.

"Oh my God." Raelyn said.

"I don't know why she always got bullshit going on." Riley said.

"See that is why I don't be with her like that." Cherry said. as the DJ got the party back going.

Riley shook her head and sent Jamir a text to make sure that he was still going to meet her at her house later that morning. He sent a text back telling her that he would be there. An hour later they counted down the new year and then they got turnt up.

Chapter 15

Riley

Jamir was waiting for Riley when she returned home. When he saw her pull up and park in front of her place, he got out of his car and followed her into her apartment. After Riley closed and locked the door, Jamir scooped her up into his arms.

"Boo you look good in this," he said as he squeezed her butt. He was speaking of the sparkly dress that she was wearing.

Riley giggled and said, "Thank you. You look good in this suit too."

"Yea I am killing this shit ain't I?" Jamir smiled.

Riley giggled as Jamir palmed her butt again.

"Damn boo did your ass get thicker?" he asked.

"Shut up." Riley said and then she hit him in the arm.

"I'm serious that ass is way fatter. I've been putting in work on that." Jamir chuckled.

Riley smacked her lips and chuckled. She knew the true reason for her butt being more plump than normal was because she had gained a little weight while she was pregnant for that brief time. Jamir still didn't know about the pregnancy and she didn't want to tell him right then because she didn't want to spoil the mood.

"Whatever babe. Come and take some shots with me for the new year." Riley said. She walked to the kitchen.

"Alright." Jamir said and then he followed her.

Riley pulled out some shot glasses and poured Patron into them.

"Happy New Year!" she said.

He repeated what she said and then they took the first one down in one swallow, and then she poured another. They took the second one down and then she poured a third one and told him to sit down on the couch, so she could get changed into her pajamas.

"Uh-uh. What are you doing? Don't take that off yet." Jamir said.

"What?"

"I want you to dance for me."

"Dance for you?" Riley laughed.

"Yea. Strip for me."

"I don't know how to dance. Jamir."

"Yes, you do baby. Just be sexy."

"I've never done nothing like that."

"This will be your first. I want to see you take that sexy shit off slow." Jamir said.

He gulped down the last shot of Patron and picked up his phone. He found the song, "B.E.D" by Jaquees and pressed play. Riley smiled, downed the last shot of Patron, and stood in front of Jamir. She let out a nervous giggled.

"Go ahead sexy do your thing."

"Ok." Riley said. She took a deep breath and then let herself get into the song and the moment. She started moving her hips slowly and seductively.

"Yea that's it right there, boo." Jamir said as he watched her.

Riley kept her eyes on him as she wound her hips and rolled her upper body backward slowly and seductively. She started doing her best version of belly dancing as she gradually unzipped the dress and slid it off her body. Riley was wearing a fishnet body suit with only a black thong underneath the dress.

"Damn." Jamir said when he saw her standing there with the fishnet body suit on and a pair of knee-high boots. He grabbed the crotch of his jeans, bit his bottom lip, and started removing the suit jacket and button up shirt he had on.

Riley rubbed her hand down her body slowly, back up, and then gently squeezed her nipples between her thumb and first finger. She then turned, bent over, and made her ass clap for him. That did it for Jamir. He reached out, grabbed her, and pulled her to him. Riley straddled

Jamir while he sucked her nipples through the fishnet. She continued to wind her hips on him until he put his lips on hers. They shared a long kiss and then Jamir stood up with Riley in his arms and carried her into the bedroom. He laid her on the bed, took his clothes off, and found the accessible hole in the middle of her body suit. He moved her panties to the side, stuffed his hard manhood inside her, and started banging into her peach. Riley wrapped her knee-high boots around him and dug her nails into his back.

"You sexy as fuck." he groaned.

"So are you." she whispered in his ear.

"This pussy good." Jamir moaned.

"Mmmm." she moaned.

"This pussy mine?"

"Yes." Riley responded.

"It better be." he said.

Jamir pulled out of her and flipped her over by one leg. He pushed himself back into her while she lay flat on her stomach and started going even harder. Riley loved it. She dug her nails into the sheets and cried out, "Jamir!"

"That D good?"

"Yes baby." Riley moaned.

"I know it is."

Jamir put his chest on her back and put his fingers into her hair. He pulled her head to the side and kissed her, sucked on her neck, and them he lifted back up. Jamir put both hands on her ass and started pounding harder.

"Mmm yes Jamir. Hit this pussy." she said loudly. She was giving him the encouragement he wanted.

"Like that?" he asked.

"Yes." she moaned.

He smacked her ass hard and Riley sunk her teeth into her sheets.

"Uuugh." She groaned as she felt every aggressive thrust Jamir was giving her.

"Right there, baby. I'm cum…" Her orgasm caught her words. "Ah!" Riley yelled out.

"Hell yea. You look sexy as fuck in this shit." Jamir said.

Before he could catch himself, Jamir matched her orgasm with one of his own. He paused while he let his seeds go inside of her and then Jamir pulled out of her. He wiped sweat from his forehead and then he leaned down and kissed her.

"Shit baby. You had me on ten. I couldn't control it." he chuckled.

Riley giggled and turned over onto her back. Jamir climbed out of bed and made his way to her bathroom.

"You're on the pill, right." he called back to her.

"Yea." Riley said.

"Aight." he said.

Riley was shocked when he came out of the bathroom with a towel for her after he finished washing up. She was even more surprised when he climbed back into the bed with her and cuddled up. Jamir kissed her on the cheek and pulled her into his arms. A feeling of excitement covered Riley.

Oh my God. He is coming around. I told everyone all I had to do is be patient. Riley thought.

"I love you." she whispered to Jamir.

"Shhhh. I know bae." he whispered before drifting off to sleep.

Did he just say bae? I'm his bae now. Riley thought. She smiled and closed her eyes.

Chapter 16

Paris

Me and my husband were lying on the couch watching television. Well, I was watching television and Laron's attention was on his phone. I laughed at the television and the I asked him, "Baby did you see that?"

"No. What?" he asked.

"Never mind you weren't paying attention."

"I was baby."

"No, you weren't."

"Ok. I wasn't. I'm sorry baby. Give me a second."

I rolled my eyes and turned my attention back to the show that was on the television. He was still looking at his phone. A second turned to minutes and then minutes turned into an hour. The show was ending, and my husband was still on his phone. He only looked up a couple of times during the show. I had an attitude by that time.

"Baby we should go out for dinner and drinks tonight."

"Nah baby I got something to do with my boys tonight. We can do that some other time."

I sat up and said, "Baby we don't go out anymore."

"Yes, we do."

"No, we don't"

"We just went to a play not too long ago."

"With Raelyn."

"So, we went to the New Year's Eve party last week."

"With Raelyn."

"Not the whole night."

"Yea, but we stopped by her party and we spent the night with her."

"Well. we just went out to dinner a few nights ago."

"With Raelyn."

"Ok. What is your point baby?"

"My point is, we never go out together anymore. The only time we go out is when we are with Raelyn."

"So, you have a problem with Raelyn now?"

"No. I'm just saying, me and you used to do everything together. When are you going to make time just for us?"

"I'm here right now Paris."

"And you're on your phone. Probably with Raelyn."

"I thought you said that you were cool with Raelyn."

"I am. I am just saying when will it be about me and you again?"

"Alright, I hear you baby. Calm down. I got you. Me and you. I promise. Just not tonight. Ok baby?"

"Ok."

"I'll be back later."

"Ok."

He stood up, kissed me, and walked out of our house to go do whatever him and his *boys* had plans to do. He didn't even tell me where he was going like he usually does. I didn't question because I typically don't have to. I sat back on the couch and picked up the remote.

Chapter 17

Raelyn

Laron was at my house again. Making love to me again for like the eighth time in two weeks. *Fuck*. I thought. I couldn't shake how I felt about him. Since the first time we had made love without his wife, he had me open. Laron touched me in all the right spots, he said the right things, and he pressed all my buttons. He made me feel things I had never felt. Laron was slowly becoming my love drug, and I couldn't get enough of him. I was convinced that I was becoming his love drug too. If I could have him all to myself, I would. After I thought about my position is his life, I was ready to walk away, but somehow, I let him talk me back into bed with him and his wife. Maybe I was like her. I was just doing it for him. I had told myself numerous times that I was doing it for fun, but I no longer knew what I was doing it for. Maybe a part of me was holding on to him by any means necessary, and if that meant being with his wife, I was willing.

Before we started having sex that day, I asked him about Paris again, and he told me again that Paris was in the know about him having sex with me without her being involved. Even though he told me that Paris didn't care, I had wondered if his wife knew that he was seeing me so frequently. Part of me wanted to call her, but I told myself to stay in my lane.

What they do as a couple is their business and whatever agreement they have with each other is between them. I thought, and then everything erased from my mind as my orgasm hit me.

"Ah Laron!" I cried out.

My voice echoed through my bedroom. He leaned down and stuck his tongue into my mouth. I put my hands into his sandy brown dreads and tongue kissed him until my orgasm subsided. After I came down from the orgasm high, Laron pounded into me until he busted. He kissed me passionately before getting up to wash up. I went into the bathroom to wash up after he was finished and then I got back into my bed next to him.

He wrapped his arms around me and said, we should run away together."

I asked, "Huh?"

"You heard me. We should run away together."

"Stop Laron."

"Stop what? I am serious."

"You can't be. You're married."

"But, I am serious."

"What are you talking about?"

"Leave here and start a new life somewhere else. Just me and you."

"Laron. You're married."

"I can be unmarried."

"Don't talk like that. You two love each other. You can't do that to Paris."

"People fall out of love."

"I don't want to be the reason that you fall out of love with her."

"What if you're not."

"I would still feel like I am."

"I hear you."

We sat there in silence for a moment and then his phone rang. Laron picked it up and answered it.

He said, "Hey. I'm coming now."

Laron hung up and looked at me. "I got to go baby. Me and Paris got some running around to do. Still on for tomorrow night with us, right?"

"Yes."

"Alright. Will you at least think about what I said?"

"Laron, stop."

"Ok. baby."

Laron kissed me, climbed out of my bed, got dressed, and left.

***

All the ladies stopped by my place later that evening for food, drinks, and girl chat. I had cooked up a delicious meal for the three of them, and I had made a nice fruity drink that I got the recipe for on Facebook. Everyone was sitting in my living room on my couches. A repeat of a reality show episode was on my television, but no one was watching it. We were too busy talking.

"Taji what was that at the New Year's Eve party?" I asked as I handed her a plate of food.

"Please do tell." Cherry chimed in.

"Girl my dude acted a fool. I'm sorry y'all."

"But, weren't you with the dude that you were cheating on him with?" I asked as I handed Cherry and Riley plates of food.

Taji said, "Yea." after taking a bite of food. "Mmm girl this is good." she said with a mouth full of food.

"It is." Cherry said.

"Thanks." I said as I sat down on the couch with my drink and plate of food.

"He wasn't supposed to be going out that night. I don't even know how he knew that I was down there. I think someone in there told him." Taji said.

"Did you post pictures online?" Cherry asked.

"Nope." Taji said between bites of food."

"Yea someone snitched on you girl." Riley said.

"I hope your brother isn't mad at me." Taji said.

"Nah, he didn't even mention it." I said before taking a bite of food. I washed it down with my fruity drink.

"It was a quick fight. The bouncers broke it up fast." Riley said.

"You should be careful with that Taji. Someone could have gotten seriously hurt." Cherry said.

"I didn't think that I was going to get caught. I ain't sloppy like dudes are."

"Uh. Ding dong alert. Coming to the club with your side dude is sloppy." Riley said.

"Yea there are too many cameras these days to be in public with your side piece. You got to keep that shit in private." I said.

"True." Taji said.

Cherry said, "You know better. You're just with that drama."

"No, I'm not."

All of us gave her the side eye.

"Why not just leave his bum ass." Cherry asked.

"I love my bae, but I got someone on the side for when he acts up."

"Does your side piece know that you have a man?" I asked.

"Yup. He doesn't care. He's been around for years. He loves me too."

"Because your giving up the cookie with no rules, restrictions, or obligations. I wouldn't care either if I was a dude." Riley said.

"I don't care what anybody says. Love triangles are not cool no matter which way you slice them up." Cherry said. "That goes for you too Rae."

My face frowned. "What? My situation is different. We are all consenting adults who are aware of each other and respect each other."

"Um hum. That is what you think."

"Ha! I told you." Riley said.

"Shut up." I said.

"No woman is just willing to share her man with another woman."

"Well, Laron's woman is."

"Is that what you think or is that what he told you?" Cherry asked.

I ignored the question. I had to change the subject to get the heat off me. I didn't want to get into a deep conversation about my relationship with Laron and Paris.

I said, "Anyways. Taji your side piece is fine by the way."

Cherry was irritated that I ignored her question, but she let it pass and jumped on to the next subject with us.

"I meant to tell you that." Cherry said.

"That body Oooo wee!" Riley said.

"And he was letting your boyfriend have it too." I said.

Taji laughed out loud, "Ahahahaha!"

"Yea he that deal in the bedroom too." Taji said.

"He looks like he is." Riley said.

"I thought you like having sex with your dude?" Cherry asked.

"He is alright. He busts too fast for me. He acts like he can't handle the pussy, but my side dude got stamina. He ain't never stopping unless I tell him too."

"Damn." Riley said.

"Um hum. That's why he will forever be my side piece."

"A shame." Cherry said and shook her head.

Nia Rich

Chapter 18

Paris

I noticed a difference in my husband. He seemed to be even more distant than he was when I complained about us not spending any time with each other, and he seemed a little bit cold. It felt like someone turned off the burner in our house. I didn't know if it was me, but he didn't seem like he was there with me mentally. My husband always seemed like he was thinking about something else when he was with me, and he wasn't at home as much anymore. He was working more, and when he was home, he seemed to always be busy, or have something to do. I thought allowing him to bring Raelyn into our bedroom was going to bring us closer. It did for a while, and then it felt like he started moving further away from me.

"Baby do you love me?" I asked from across the dinner table in a dimly lit restaurant.

Laron looked up from his phone and said, "Yes. Why would you ask me that?"

"Because you just don't seem that into me right now. I've been staring at you looking at your phone for over ten minutes now, and we are at dinner together. You haven't once looked at me."

"Baby I'm sorry. I don't mean to make you feel that way. I didn't realize that I wasn't paying attention to you. I was hollering at a potential client about a photoshoot. Forgive me."

He gave me the puppy dog eyes he always gave me when I was irritated or angry about something. I exhaled and then I said, "It feels like ever since Raelyn came into our lives. Things have changed."

"Here you go again about this Raelyn stuff. I don't know why you feel like that baby."

"Because you don't see me anymore. The only time you see me is when we are in the bedroom with her, and I'm starting to wonder if you even see me then. I saw the look in your eyes while you were having sex with her the last couple of times we hooked up with her. I know that look because it's the same way you used to look at me when we first got together."

"Baby. You are thinking way too far into it. I don't know what look you're talking about. The only woman I see is you. Ok? I love you. Stop tripping."

I pursed my lips and looked at the waitress coming our way. I said, "Ok."

"Look. I'm putting the phone down. You have all of my attention beautiful."

I smiled at him, but I wasn't feeling it. He promised me a body massage after dinner, so maybe he will convince me then.

***

My husband kissed my feet as he rubbed them with massage oil. He was giving me a full body massage by candle light. We had some love making music playing in the background. He had already made his way down the front of my body, and was focusing on my feet. I smiled as he sucked a few of my toes. He told me to turn over onto my stomach. He rubbed my shoulders, back, arms, butt, and legs. When he reached my feet again, he kissed and sucked on them, and then I felt him trail his tongue back up my thighs. I moaned as I felt him getting closer to my juice box. He spread my cheeks first and dipped his tongue inside. He did a few tongue tricks between my cheeks. My mouth opened a little and a few soft moans escaped.

He stopped and said, "Raise your hips baby."

I raised up into a doggy style position. Laron put his mouth on my lower lips from the back. He was sucking on my juice box like it was the best flavor he'd ever tasted. My husband didn't stop until my waterfall was dripping all over his lips and tongue. After his amazing oral pleasure, my body was craving him. I begged him to put himself inside me. My husband dipped his finger inside of my waterfall a few times, and then he took his boxers off and slid inside of my wetness. I couldn't remember the last time we'd made love to each other without our third party, and I was happy to be alone with him again. I made sexy sounds and let him work me from the back.

"Ah yes right there." I moaned. I begin getting into the groove with him by bouncing back.

He asked, "That's the spot?"

"Yes." I moaned and then I heard him whisper, "Raelyn."

I stopped. "What?" I asked with an attitude.

He looked confused. "What? Why did you stop?"

"What did you just say?" I asked. I moved and turned around to look at him. I folded my arms across my chest.

"I don't know what you are talking about." he said.

"You know what I am talking about Laron! You just called me Raelyn's name during sex."

"No, I didn't that is not what I said." he said. My husband wiped his sweaty forehead with his hand.

"Yes, it is Laron! I can't believe you!"

"Baby, you're tripping for real." He reached for me.

"Don't fucking touch me! I don't want to do that shit with her no more!" I yelled. I got out of bed, walked into the bathroom, slammed the door, and locked it. My husband followed me to the bathroom and wiggled the handle. When he realized that the door was locked, he started talking to me through the door.

"Baby, please open the door."

"NO! Go away Laron!"

"Baby, please listen. I didn't say her name I promise baby."

"Well what did you say!?"

"I don't know baby please open the door."

"No! Just leave me alone Laron!"

He pounded on the door with his open hand a few times and then he said, "Ok."

My husband walked away and walked downstairs to the living room. That is where he slept that night. I stayed in the bathroom until I stopped crying, and then I crawled into bed by myself. My husband returned to our bedroom early the next morning and crawled into bed next to me.

Chapter 19

Raelyn

After I hooked up with Laron and Paris another time, I decided that it was going to be the last time. My twin sister Riley was right. Doing things with them had gotten old and there wasn't any future in it. Plus, the way Paris was acting the last time we got together, felt like she wasn't that into it. I wasn't in to it either. I was ready for something more. I asked Laron to meet me for a lunch date, so I could tell him that I wanted to end it. I picked a restaurant in uptown that had a nice happy hour. He came in looking and smelling good as usual. He had his dreads pulled back into a ponytail and a pair of clear glasses on.

"Hey baby." Laron said when he reached the table.

I stood up to hug him and said, "Thanks for meeting me."

"Anytime baby. How are you?"

"I am doing good. How are you?"

"I'm great now that I am seeing you."

I smiled and told the waitress to give us a minute to look through the menu when she approached our table.

"I'm leaving town tomorrow. I know that you don't work during the week, so I was hoping that you would come with me."

"You and Paris?"

"No, just me and you."

"Well that is what I wanted to talk to you about."

"What's up?"

"I'm going to take a step back from dealing with you and Paris."

"Are you trying to break up with us?"

"Basically. Yes. Don't misunderstand. I really enjoyed myself with you two, but being your third party is not something that I want anymore."

Laron nodded his head, licked his lips, and asked, "Well what about us?"

"We've already talked about that. I have developed strong feelings for you, and I think that it's best for me to leave you alone completely. The reality is, I can't have you, and I feel that it is time for me to find a love of my own."

"Baby. I already told you that I don't want to be with her anymore. I want to be with you."

"But you are still very married to her, so you should figure that out with her and then after that is done we can talk about us, but I am not going to wait, and I don't want to be your reason for leaving her."

"Raelyn will you at least think about it?"

"I already have and I am set with this decision."

He sighed and said, "Alright."

The waitress came back to our table and I told her that we decided not to order. Both of us stood up and walked out of the restaurant together. He hugged me before I got into my car and drove off.

Chapter 20

Paris

I took a puff from my cigarette and blew it in the air. I looked down some old cigarette butts on the ground.

"Uh-oh what got you smoking girl?" Priscilla asked. She had met me at a café for lunch and girl chat. I was outside smoking when she pulled up.

"Laron." I said and then I took another puff.

She asked, "What did he do?"

I blew smoke into the air, and then I said, "He called me another woman's name during sex."

Priscilla's mouth fell open and she covered it with one of her hands. "He didn't do that." she said after taking her hand away from her mouth.

"Yes, he did, and I have been pissed about it since."

"Whose name did he call you?"

"The chick that we've been having a threesome with." I said.

She shook her head. "I tried to tell you about doing stuff like that."

"I know. I know."

"That's why I don't get into stuff like that because somehow it always goes wrong."

"To top it all off. He's been distant lately. He hasn't been at home a lot, and I don't know what is wrong with him."

"Has he been with her?"

"You think?"

"I don't know. He could be."

"He better not be. Because if he is, somebody is going to need a casket."

"Dang girl. I have never heard you talk like that before."

I exhaled releasing smoke from my lungs. "Don't listen to me girl I am just in my feelings right now and I am sure that I'm over thinking it."

"How many times were you two with her." she asked.

I flicked the ash from my cigarette on the ground and said, "So many times, that I can't count. We've been with her so much, she is practically our girlfriend. After he called me her name, I told him that I didn't want to do it anymore."

"Good for you. So, the question is, did Laron break it off with her?"

"I don't know, but when he comes back into town I am going to ask him.

I threw the butt of my cigarette on the ground, and then we walked into the restaurant

***

I heard Laron's car pull up and then drive into our garage. I was standing on the back porch smoking a cigarette. I blew smoke in the air and flicked the ash over the balcony into the grass. I heard Laron call my name when he walked into the house, but I didn't respond to him. I listened to him walk through the house looking for me until he decided to come to the back porch. He looked out the window. When he saw me standing out there, he opened the door and stepped out.

"Hey baby. You didn't hear me calling you?"

"Yes, but I didn't want to let smoke into the house."

"I see. Why are you smoking baby?"

"You know why."

"Baby that was a while ago. Why are you still tripping on that?"

"Because babe. It was disrespectful."

"Baby. It was an accident, and I have already apologized for it." I blew smoke in the opposite direction of his face.

"Were you fantasizing about her while you were having sex with me?" I asked.

"What?"

"Answer the question."

"This is crazy."

My husband shook his head back and forth.

"You can't answer the question? You were, weren't you?"

He stopped shaking his head and said, "No."

"You're lying. That is so hurtful."

I blew smoke from the last hit from my cigarette and then I put it out in the ashtray sitting on the wood banister.

"Baby I would never fantasize about another woman while making love to you. I made a mistake and I apologize. You can't blame me for the slip up. We've been having sex with her for a while."

I folded my arms in front of my chest. "Did you break it off with her?"

"Yes, baby I did. Right before I left for Atlanta. I told her that we would no longer be hooking up with her, and I told her not to call anymore."

"So, we are done with this whole threesome thing?"

"Yes, it's just me and you." he said.

I wish I would have known then that he was lying, but I fell for it hook, line, and sinker.

I smiled. "Thank you, baby. I love you."

"I love you more."

I reached out to hug him. He accepted my hug and then he kissed me. We walked back into the house. We made love like we were doing it for the first time. I was happy to have my husband back.

Chapter 21

Raelyn

I looked at my phone ringing and pressed end. It sent the call straight to voicemail. I put the phone back into my back pocket.

"Whose call are you ignoring sister?" Riley asked.

"Laron's."

"He's calling you again?"

"Yes, he hasn't stopped calling for the past couple of weeks."

"He is not taking your break up well." she said.

"He keeps asking if we can talk, but there is no point."

"There really isn't." she said.

"We can talk until our faces turn blue, but the fact still remains. He is married."

"Wait. We are still talking about you, him, and his wife?" she asked.

"No. The last time I talked to him, he told me that he didn't want to be with his wife anymore and he wanted to be with me."

My sister raised her eyebrows and said, "Whoa."

I said, "I know. I told him that I wouldn't be the reason that he leaves her."

"What if he does leave her? Would you be with him?"

"I told him that we could talk about it then, but who knows, I might be with someone else by then. I can't lie sister. I do miss him."

"You miss him? Or you miss the dick?"

I laughed, "Shut up. Both."

She laughed. I opened the door to the club so she could go in first. I followed her through the club to the back. Shawn was back there. It was clear to me and everyone that worked there that he liked me. He was a cool guy, but he wasn't really my type.

"Sup Twins?" Shawn asked.

Both of us spoke to him and began putting our things into a locker.

"I like your Prince T-shirt Raelyn where did you get it?" he asked.

"I ordered it online." I said.

"I got to get one. I was too sad when bruh passed." he said.

"I was too. Me and Riley stood downtown in front of First Avenue with everyone the day he passed, and then we went out to his home Paisley Park and put flowers in front of it."

"Aw y'all are some devoted fans."

"Yes sir." Riley said.

Shawn laughed.

"What y'all doing tonight?" he asked.

"I'm not doing anything. Are you sister?"

"No. Why?"

"Because it's my birthday and a few of us are going out to eat after work. I would like for y'all to come."

"Happy Birthday." we said in unison, and then I said, "I'm down, are you down sister?"

Riley said, "Yep."

"Aight cool. We are just going uptown."

"We wouldn't miss it." Riley said.

She hugged him before walking out of the back room. I hugged him and then I finished putting my things away. After Riley left, it was just me and Shawn back there alone. If I was thinking, I would have bounced when Riley did, but I set myself up for what was coming next by staying back there.

"So, Raelyn. I've been wanting to ask you if you have a man?"

"Oh, you have huh?" I smiled.

"Yes."

"Well I don't." I said.

"What happened to that guy that comes in here to see you?"

"Dang you're all up in my business. How did you know he was coming to see me?"

Shawn chuckled. "Because I saw him talking to you."

"Well, he was not my man. He was just a friend."

"Oh ok. Well, I would like to hang out with you sometime. Like, you know, go out to lunch or dinner or something."

I made a screwed face. "Are you asking me out on a date Shawn?"

He laughed. "Yes I am. I've been wanting to for a while."

I wanted to say no, but I couldn't turn a man down on his birthday. I am sure it took a lot of courage for him to ask me.

I smiled and replied, "Aw that's cute. Nah I'm just playing. Yes, I would love to go on a date with you."

"Aight cool. Can I get your number, so I can hit you up?"

"Sure." I said. He handed me his phone, so I could lock my number in.

"Cool. Well, I will see you and your sister later."

"Ok."

I walked out of the backroom and back into the club.

***

Late night breakfast with our co-workers was a blast. It was nothing but laughs at our table as we recalled various funny situations that happened over the time we'd been working at the club with each other. I was extremely tired when I pulled up to my apartment building. The sun was coming up and I was ready to take a shower, so I could get into bed and go to sleep. I parallel parked my car, got out and walked towards my door.

"Raelyn." Laron said from behind me. He startled me, so I jumped a little.

"What are you doing here?" I asked.

He closed his car door and walked over to me.

"You know I couldn't stay away for long. I wanted to talk to you."

"How long have you been out here?"

"For a couple of hours. I thought you would be coming home earlier. I was just about to leave when I saw you pull up."

Right then, I cursed myself for being too lazy to park in the underground garage.

"What do you want?" I asked.

"I miss you. I've been sick without you Rae."

"I miss you too, but you already know the situation."

"That's what I want to talk to you about. Can I come in?" he asked. I was too tired to fight.

I exhaled loudly and then I said, "Come on."

Laron followed me into my apartment building and up the stairs to my apartment. Once we were inside, he sat down on my couch.

"Make yourself at home. I need to take a quick shower before we talk. Is that alright?"

"Yea."

I went into bathroom and took shower. I put on some 'don't touch me panties and pajamas', and then I rejoined Laron in my living room, so we could talk.

I sat down and said, "What's up?"

"I want to be with you."

"Laron we've already talked about this."

"Here me out. I'm leaving her. Not because of you, but because I don't want to be with her anymore."

"Because of me." I said.

"Because I was already losing interest in her before you. That is why I wanted a threesome. She wasn't giving me what I wanted, so I thought having you would spice it up a little and make it more interesting."

"Why not just leave if you weren't happy?"

"I wanted to make it work, but then I met you, and you showed me something different. You give me everything I want and need."

I leaned my head back on my couch and looked up at the ceiling. "It's too much."

He put his hand on my thigh. "All you need to know is that I love and miss you."

When I felt his hand on my thigh, my mind started screaming no, but my body was saying yes. I closed my eyes when I felt his lips on my neck. I knew that I no longer had control. He had control and that is what I was running from for the few weeks that I hadn't talked to him. The feeling of his lips on my skin he gave me let me know that my 'don't touch me' pajamas were not working.

I felt his lips kiss around my color bone. I felt his hand slide up my shirt, his fingers squeeze and gently rub my nipples. My kitty purred. He put his lips on mine and somewhere between the passionate kiss and his intimate touches, my pajamas were removed and thrown to the floor. His face was between my legs and he was giving me that A1 oral pleasure that he always gave me.

I was moaning, arching my back, and releasing my juices onto his lips and chin. After I got mine, he undressed and dove inside of me. I was wet and ready to receive him. When I told him to go deeper, he spread my legs as far as they could go and pounded into me hard and deep. I begged for more. I told him to go harder. He grunted and pounded aggressively. My kitty made sounds for him. I matched his sounds with sounds of my own. He pounded, he grinded, he long stroked, and he short stroked. He hit my spot repeatedly until I got my O again.

"I'm cuming baby." I moaned loudly. I released my juices onto him again.

Laron kissed me while pounding me slow, and then he sped up the pace. He froze and then he pulled out. He kissed me until his manhood went soft, and then we got up and took a shower together.

Chapter 22

Paris

It was the third night in a row that Laron was out until the wee hours of the morning. He said that he had a few freelance jobs for rap artists and had to be in the night clubs doing photography. The first night was the worst because he didn't come home until eight o'clock in the morning. The second night was close to six o'clock in the morning. I was so beside myself that I had the nerve to call Raelyn looking for my husband. She said that she hadn't seen him. I felt so dumb after talking to her that I told myself that I would never do it again. At least it was a little after four a.m. this night.

"I hope this is the last gig you have." I said when he climbed into bed.

"It is baby. I made some good money though. Tax free cash in our pockets. You feel me?"

I giggled. "Yes."

"I'm gonna take you shopping tomorrow."

"Ok."

"I know that makes you happy don't it."

"Yes." I smiled.

He kissed me on the shoulder and pulled me into his arms. I turned over and put my hands on is manhood.

"Naw baby. Not tonight. I am too tired. I've been on my feet for hours."

I frowned. "When have you ever been too tired?" I asked.

"Baby. Don't fuss. I'm tired. Tomorrow ok?" he said with his eyes already closed.

He was sleep a few seconds later. I frowned and then I sat up in the bed. I was pissed and horny and I couldn't do anything about it. I've never been into masturbation. I just wanted the man that I loved to make love to me and he was lying next to me snoring. I couldn't sleep, so I picked up the remote and turned on the television.

***

It was morning and I had been up all night. I figured that I would be a good wife and wake him up the right way, and then maybe he would be in the mood to make love to me. I slid underneath our comforter and pulled his soft and squishy flesh out of his boxers. I put it into my mouth and gently sucked on him until I felt him start to swell.

He moved a little and then he said, "What are you doing baby?"

"I'm making you feel good." I said between sucks and licks.

"Mmm damn baby." he said.

He started pumping in and out of my mouth while I bobbed my head up and down on his hard manhood. He got into it while I did my thing, and then I let him bust in my mouth for the first time. I didn't swallow. I spit his man juice back onto his manhood as I continued to suck him back into softness. I got up and walked to the bathroom. I brushed my teeth and wet a wash cloth. I went back to my husband and cleaned him up.

"That's how you feel this morning?" he asked.

"Yes."

"You have never woken me up with head in the morning."

"It was time for something different."

"That shit was good."

I smiled, "Are you hungry?"

"Yes, baby I am."

"I am going downstairs to make you breakfast."

My husband smiled. I headed downstairs to start breakfast for the man that I loved. It was time to restore the normalcy in our marriage. I pulled pots and pans out of the cabinets, and then I pulled bowls and other utensils out of the kitchen drawers. I got busy making pancakes, eggs, and bacon for my husband. He came downstairs and walked up to me standing in front of the stove. He hugged me from behind, kissed me on the shoulder and my neck. I could smell freshness from toothpaste on his breath.

"You are too good to me woman." he whispered.

"That's because I love you."

"I love you too baby."

"Go have a seat. The food will be ready soon."

I finished making breakfast and joined Laron at the table. We ate and talked about current events. The club night event he did the night before, and the business trip he was taking to do a photoshoot. I told him that I had a modeling gig coming as well in California and that I was going to visit my family while I was there. He told me that he could meet me there that weekend after he finished his gig. After we finished breakfast, he helped me clear our plates. He put his plate and glass into the sink, and then he grabbed me by the waist and pulled me to him. He kissed me, picked me up, and put me onto the counter.

"I'm still hungry." he said as he opened my satin robe and removed my panties. I smiled at him. He was giving me what I wanted. He reached in the refrigerator and pulled out a bottle of whipped cream.

"What are you doing?"

"Something different like you said. I told you I was still hungry. You are about to be my desert."

I squealed and laughed when I felt the cold cream on my thighs. He put whipped cream down the middle of thighs and on my peach.

"Peaches and cream." he said.

He put the can on the counter next to us and then sucked and licked his way down my thigh to my peach. He sucked and licked on my pearl removing every drop of the whipped cream from my peach. I was losing it the whole time. I couldn't control my sounds. My husband was in control and he had me in another world.

"Uuuuuuh, baby yes, don't stop. Stay right there, stay ri—"

My orgasm cut my sentence short. I threw my head back and squealed, "Baby! Ahh yes!"

As my orgasm rocked me, he put whipped cream on my nipples. He watched me lose it some more as he sucked the cold cream off my nipples, and then he slid my butt to the edge of the counter, and put his stiff manhood inside of me. He made me wait all night, and I was craving the feeling of him inside of me. As he pumped in and out of me, I grinded onto his thick girth with aggression. I was chasing that O. I wanted to feel it again, but with him inside of me. That is the kind of orgasm I like the most. He found my spot and stayed on it.

I moaned, "Yes, yes, yes. Right there."   as he pumped his manhood into me.

"That's it?"

"Um hum."

My husband pounded harder into my spot. I squealed again and released my waterfall onto him. He smiled, pulled out and stepped back. He told me to get down. I put my feet on the ground, and then he turned me around and entered me from behind. He wrapped my hair around his hand and put his pound game on me against the counter until he busted.

Chapter 23

Paris

I hooked up with my best friend Priscilla later that day just to chat. She had the day off work and we decided to head to mall. We walked around the amusement park that sits in the middle of the gigantic mall. We were taking a short cut to the other side.

Priscilla asked, "So, you and the hubby are back on good terms? I see that you are not smoking any cigarettes."

"I guess you can say that." I said.

"You guess?" she asked.

"Yea. We are cool, but something still just doesn't feel right. Even the sex is different."

"What's different?"

"I don't know. He is there, and he is doing it, but it feels like he isn't there mentally, or maybe he isn't as into it as before. I don't know maybe I am over thinking it."

"You're not. That is women's intuition. We know when, something isn't right."

"It's like his mind is somewhere else. Like we had sex this morning, and he gave me the best oral ever, but he didn't look me in my eyes once. He didn't tell me that it was good or moan my name like he used to. It was like he was just doing it to please me so I won't complain. Like he was pacifying me or something."

"Only you know your husband's sexual patterns."

"Right. I also feel like he's lying to me. He's been out later than usual supposedly working, and I am trying to be understanding, but I am losing my patience. Even the Valentine's day didn't feel the same. He seemed like he would've had rather been somewhere else than to be spending them with me and my family. Now it's early April, and it has been months since we stopped having our threesomes. I still don't believe that he is always where he says he is."

"Could it be that girl?"

"I don't think so, she doesn't call anymore that I know of. At least I haven't heard him on the phone with her. I called her one night and she said that she hadn't seen or talked to him, but that was a while ago. I feel like it could be another chick. I wish I could get into his phone."

"Why don't you put a GPS tracker on his phone?" Priscilla asked.

"You can do that?"

"Yes girl. I thought you knew that?"

"No. I am in the dark about that."

"Yea, well, it will tell you where he is at, if you feel like he may be on something sneaky. I did it to my ex-boyfriend, and I caught him at the movies with a chick. Let me tell you, it was a bad scene."

"I am going to consider that. Girl if I find him with Raelyn or another chick, I might be going to prison for life."

Priscilla laughed and said, "There you go again talking crazy."

I chuckled a little and said, "I know. I am just in my feelings again girl."

Chapter 24

Riley

Riley looked over at Jamir who had his eyes on the television. They were having drinks and watching a basketball game at her house that night. Riley put her eyes back on the television, but her mind was elsewhere. She was thinking about their relationship. It had been almost a year, but Jamir hadn't mentioned being together. He called her by a pet name. He was at her house all the time. Sex was amazing with him. She cooked for him, and practically did anything he asked. She'd even been bringing him lunch to his job every day, and his uncle seemed like he liked her. Riley couldn't figure out what else Jamir could've possibly wanted. In her mind, they were practically in a relationship.

She just wanted him to give her the title of being his woman, so she could introduce him to her parents, move in together, and hopefully get married.

Riley asked, "Jamir what are we doing?"

"We are watching the game."

"No. That is not what I am talking about. I'm talking about us. What are we doing? Where is this relationship going?"

"Don't start that shit again Riley."

"I need to know."

"Need to know what? Bae, you already know. You are my bae. We are chilling. We are good. I'm over here all the time ain't I?"

"Yes. I know, but I love you Jamir and I want to be together. I want to be your woman."

"See here you go with the drama. You know I don't like titles Riley. We don't need a title baby. You know I care deeply for you, and we good baby."

"Jamir, it has been almost a year."

He sighed and rubbed his beard "Oh man. Why are you doing this right now Riley. We are watching the game. We are chilling, alright bae?"

He pulled her chin to him and kissed her. He put his hand between her legs and rubbed her peach and said, "I know what you want. I'm going to give it to you when this game is over, alright?"

Riley smiled and pushed his hand away. "Stop. I don't want that."

"Yes, you do." Jamir smiled. "Every time you get to tripping that is exactly what you want. This D will get you back straight."

Riley laughed, put her head on his shoulder, and finished watching the game.

***

Jamir had Riley bent over in doggy style position in her bed watching his manhood disappear and reappear from Riley's wet center while recording it on his phone.

"Look at that shit." he said. As he watched Riley put on a show for him. She was bouncing her ass and making it clap while he was deep stroking her.

"That's right. Come here and get this nut." Riley pulled off his manhood and crawled to him. She put him into her mouth and sucked him while on camera again. Riley sucked her juices off him and then he recorded himself release onto her face. She took it and smiled.

"That shit good for your skin." he said.

"I know." Riley replied on camera.

Jamir laughed, stopped recording, and said, "You nasty, girl."

Riley giggled and said, "You like it."

"I do."

"That means you are just as nasty as I am." Riley said as she walked to the bathroom to clean her face.

She used a separate towel to wash her box, and then she walked back into the bedroom with a wet wash cloth for Jamir. She cleaned him while he put his phone on the charger. She put the wash cloth in the bathroom.

"I love you." she said to him when she returned to the bed.

"I know. Now come lay down and watch this with me."

He found the video they had made in his phone and played it back.

"We look sexy." she said.

"Every time. Look at your face right here. See the look in your eyes while you are sucking me? That's what I love."

"Oh, you love me sucking you, but you don't love me?"

"Hush bae that is not what I said."

"You never say that you love me."

"Riley why are you trying to mess up this moment?"

"I'm not."

"Ok well stop. You know I got love for you and you know I care about you a lot. You're my bae for real."

"I'm you're bae?"

"You know that."

Riley smiled and cuddled up next to him. She started rubbing his manhood as they watched the sex video on his phone. When she felt him stiffen she dipped her head under the covers and put his manhood into her mouth again. This time doing it slower and more sensual than on the video. Riley wanted Jamir to feel how much she loved him and then maybe he would give her the title that she wanted. Riley heard Jamir started moaning. He began grinding himself into her mouth while watching them on his phone.

"Damn Riley you give the best head." he moaned.

Riley licked the head and then stuffed him all back into her mouth. She was feeling it and so was Jamir. He set the phone down next to him and closed his eyes, but then a loud banging at the door broke both of their focus.

"What's that?" Jamir asked.

"I don't know." Riley said. She crawled from under the covers.

She said, "I hope we weren't too loud and disturbed my neighbors."

"It has been a long time since they have pounded on the ceiling because of us."

"I know."

Boom. Boom. Boom. Ding Dong.

"What the fuck. Who is pounding and ringing the doorbell like that at one o'clock in the morning." Riley said as she slid out of bed and put on her robe. She walked to the door to see who or what it was. She opened the top door and tip toed down to the bottom door.

"Who is it?" she called out.

"Tell my husband to come outside bitch! I know he is in there!" A woman's voice yelled through the heavy wooden door.

Riley peeped out the curtain. A tall brown skinned woman was standing outside. She had her hair in a ponytail, a sweat suit on, and some Reebok sneakers on her feet. Riley had never seen the woman before. She didn't know who she was.

Riley said, "I'm sorry, but you have the wrong house."

"NO! I have the right place! Tell my husband Jamir to bring his raggedy ass outside!" The woman yelled.

Riley closed the blinds and frowned. "What?" she asked herself.

The woman pounded on the door again harder, ringing the doorbell more, and she started yelling louder.

BOOM! BOOM! BOOM! Ding Dong, Ding Dong, Ding Dong.

"I'M GOING TO BEAT YOUR ASS BITCH! OPEN THIS DOOR OR I'M GOING TO KICK IT DOWN!"

Riley turned and marched back up the wooden stairs. "Jamir! Some woman is at my door yelling for you to come outside! She said she is your wife!"

Jamir's eye's bulged open. He jumped out of Riley's bed and began getting dressed.

"Your wife Jamir!? Really!?" Riley yelled at him.

"Not now Riley." he said as he walked towards the door. Riley followed him through her house.

"WHAT DO YOU MEAN NOT NOW!? YOU'RE WIFE IS AT MY DOOR AND YOU'RE TRYING TO SHUSH ME!?" Riley yelled at his back.

Jamir walked down the stairs and looked out the blinds. Riley stood at the top of the stairs and watched with her arms folded across her chest.

"Jamir open this fucking door now!" The woman yelled.

"Kiesha what are you doing here!?"

"What the hell are you doing here at one o'clock in the morning Jamir! You told me that you were at your mom's house liar!"

"Kiesha leave now!" he yelled through the door.

"I'm not leaving until you come out!"

"I'm going to call the police Kiesha! Go Home!"

"You're going to call the police on me!? Fuck you, alright! Call them! I don't fucking care!"

BOOM!

Kiesha kicked the door and then stepped back and kicked it again.

BOOM!

Riley said, "Both of y'all need to go! You are disturbing my neighbors! Get out!"

"Riley I'm not trying to argue with you too!" Jamir said.

"You don't have to! You just need to get out of my house before my neighbors call the police!" Jamir stormed back up the stairs to Riley's apartment to put on the rest of his clothes.

Riley followed him with her arms still folded. She was so pissed she couldn't even find the words to say to him. Jamir snatched his phone and wallet off her night stand and put it into his pocket. Riley followed him back down the stairs. She stood on the steps to wait for him to go out so she could close and lock her door. Riley knew that she would need to talk to her neighbors the next day to apologize for all the commotion.

Jamir opened the door to walk out and then his wife pushed past him and attacked Riley. Kiesha started swinging on Riley connecting a few punches before Riley could react to what was happening. Riley wasn't much of a fighter, so she did her best windmill punching as Kiesha grabbed a hold of her hair. Kiesha had a grip on Riley's hair and was punching her in the head repeatedly. Jamir used all his strength to get Kiesha off Riley. Once he got Keisha to release her grip, Jamir yanked her back out to the porch.

"What the fuck is your problem!?" Jamir yelled at Kiesha.

"You're my fucking problem!" she yelled.

"Fuck you bitch!" Riley yelled as she held her head and try to pull herself back together. Jamir was holding Kiesha back. He began pushing Keisha towards her car. Riley's neighbors had come outside to help break up the fight when they heard the commotion. Riley couldn't see who was all out there because her focus was on Keisha who had lunged at her again. Jamir grabbed Keisha and started pulling her off the porch again. Riley's neighbor stepped in front of Riley to protect her from Keisha.

"Ma'am you need to go." he said.

Kiesha dropped a patch of Riley's hair onto the porch and said, "There's your hair bitch! You better stay the fuck away from my husband! I'm gonna beat your ass on sight every time I see you!" she yelled.

"Get in the car Keisha!" Jamir yelled when he heard sirens coming their way.

Keisha got into her car and sped off making her tires screech against the street.

Jamir ran back up to the porch to check on Riley. "Are you ok."

"Get away from me Jamir!" Riley yelled.

"I'm sorry." he said.

"Sir I think you should leave. The cops are on the way." The man from downstairs said.

Jamir walked away, got into his car, and pulled off.

"Are you ok?" The man from downstairs asked Riley.

"Yes." Riley said while wiping tears from her eyes.

"I apologize for all this. I did not mean to disturb you." she said.

"No. It's ok. It's not your fault." The nice gentleman said.

Riley had never seen him before that night. The downstairs apartment was always so quiet. She knew that people lived there, but she never seen them coming or going. She could see that he was older than her but nice looking. He was wearing a black a U of M t-shirt and some grey sweat pants. His arms looked like he did a little working out. Not enough where they were bulging, but enough to show that they were shapely.

"I'm sorry. We've never met. My name is Riley. I hate to meet under these circumstances. I am so embarrassed. Please apologize to your wife for me."

"There's no wife. It's just me sweetheart."

The police pulled up and walked up to them.

"We got a call?" One of the officers said.

"Yes, I called. She was in a fight with her boyfriend and another young lady." The man from downstairs said. He stepped back so the cops could talk to Riley. When the cops left, he told Riley to knock on his door if she needed him, and then he returned to his apartment.

Chapter 25

Paris

I put the last dish in the dishwasher and turned it on. My husband walked down the stairs and met me in the kitchen. He was dressed to take me out. He looked good with his dreads twisted back into a creative style. He had on a button up shirt tucked into a pair of pants, an expensive pair of dress shoes, and his favorite clear lens frames on his face.

"Hey baby." he said before kissing me. "Are you ready to go?"

"Yes." I said.

I followed him out of the house after setting the alarm. It took us about twenty minutes to get to the restaurant. I was trying to be as calm as possible, but inside I was boiling. Not only had I put a GPS tracking device on his phone, but I'd figured out a way to get into his text messages and emails. I've read messages to and from Raelyn about how much they love each other. My husband told me that it was all sexual with Raelyn. He never said anything about loving her, or having sex with her without me. The whole time I wanted to believe that he was telling me the truth even though my gut said different. He had been at home acting like everything was normal. Then, to find out that he had been seeing her behind my back after he had told me that is was over with her. Everything in me wanted to fuck both them up, but I decided to give my husband a chance to come clean without telling him what I knew.

He was taking me to dinner that night. I was leaving for California the next morning to do a couple of photoshoots for a women's clothing catalog and online store. I planned to ask my husband some questions at dinner. We were awkwardly silent in the car on the way to the restaurant. Usually we would have been chatting away, but not that night. I could tell he had something on his mind. I had something on mind too. I wondered if he could tell. Once we were seated at the table, he pulled out his phone and sent a text message and then he put his phone in his pocket and gave me his full attention.

"I forgot to say that you look beautiful baby."

"Thank you. You know that you look handsome as always."

"Thank you."

"What time do you leave out for New York tomorrow?" I asked.

He replied, "A couple of hours after you leave for California."

"Are you still meeting me out there?"

"Oh absolutely. You know I got to be there to support my wife and to make sure that the photographer knows what he is doing. Are you excited to see your family baby?"

"Of course, I am." I smiled.

The waiter poured water in our glasses, took our orders, and walked away. After the waiter walked away, I put my plan into action. Operation: Make Laron Confirm

His Lies. I had already heard them before, so I don't know why I needed more confirmation. I guess it was just one of the stupid things we women do when we're in love with a man. I didn't want to believe it. I wanted so bad to be just tripping. I wanted to not want to smack the shit out of him. I wanted to believe that I had gotten myself all riled up for nothing, so our lives could go back to normal. I wished that I had never seen the text messages, the emails, and the tracking info that I gathered from his phone.

I cleared my throat and then I asked, "Um my mom asked about you yesterday. I told her you that were with your cousin, right?"

"Yes, I was. Tell your mom I said hi." he said.

That was lie number one. I knew that he wasn't with his cousin because his GPS tracker told me that.

"I will." I said.

The waiter sat our food on the table, and we began to eat.

I swallowed a bite of my food and then I asked, "I ran across Raelyn's page on Facebook. She looks happy. Have you talked to her?"

"No. Not at all baby. Not since I broke up with her." he said without hesitation. Not even a flinch.

That was lie number two. I wanted to snatch him up over the table. According to his text messages, he talks to her every day. At all times of the day, but he was in my face acting like he had nothing to do with her.

"I saw a receipt in your car from a pleasure shop. What was that for?"

"Oh baby. I brought you something. I wanted to try something new, but then I decided you weren't going to like it, so I took it back." he said and took a bite of his food.

"Oh ok." I said.

That was lie number three. He knew damn well that I don't like freaky shit like toys, so he knew not to buy me anything like that. He brought it for that trash box Raelyn.

"What is with all these questions babe."

"I'm just chatting with you." I said.

"Oh ok."

I took a deep breath and held my composure, but I was pissed. I felt my hand start shaking, so I excused myself from the table to go to the ladies' room to calm down.

"Excuse me." I said angrily.

"What's wrong? Where are you going baby?"

"I'm going to the bathroom. I'll be right back."

Chapter 26

Raelyn

I heard my phone ringing again and I knew that it was my sister, but Laron was in the middle of putting chocolate syrup all over my toes to suck it off. Riley had called me the night before, but I was with Laron, so I didn't answer. I watched Laron sucking my toes like they were the best ice cream sundae he's ever eaten. I promised myself that I would call my sister back after I got the best sex ever from Laron.

I smiled at Laron as he was gently massaging my toes with his mouth and tongue.

"You like that don't you baby?" Laron asked.

"Yes, I do." I replied. He finished sucking the chocolate off my toes and begin kissing up my legs towards my juice box.

"I bought you a new toy." he said.

I smiled and said, "Really?"

"Yep. It has three different speeds and ten different pulse settings. I figured it should keep you busy when I am not around."

"Awww thank you baby." I said.

"You're welcome. I'll give it to you before I leave tomorrow." he said and then he kissed my thigh.

I said, "New York should be amazing."

"Yup as soon as you get there. You got the ticket I bought you?"

"Yes. They are in a safe place."

"Good. I'm glad that you decided to come and spend a couple of days with me. Don't forget, I got a shoot to do in Cali when we leave N.Y. so I will meet you back here in Minnesota when that is done."

"When do I get to see your new place?"

"As soon as I finish furnishing it. I got a court date when I get back to finalize this divorce and then I am all yours."

I smiled before saying, "I should tell you now. I think that I may be pregnant." I knew that I had just casually hit him with a bombshell, but there was no better time like the present.

Laron paused and looked at me. "What?" he asked.

I said, "Yes. My period is late."

"Oh, wow baby."

He gave me a nervous smile and scratched his head.

"I know. I felt the same way. I mean, I know that you are going through a divorce, so if you don't want to keep it I understand."

"No baby, I would never tell you to do that."

"When do you find out?"

"I planned to take a test before flying out to New York."

"Alright, well let me know. Either way, you're my baby and we are going to be each other's soon. I got you."

"Ok." I said.

I smiled and watched him bury his head between my legs. I tilted my head back and let him take me to another place with his mouth and tongue.

***

My bed felt so much better with Laron in it. I loved having him around and thoughts about a future with him had been swirling around in my mind. I wasn't thinking about a baby, but being with Laron everyday was something that I was growing excited about.

After we made love, we passed out in each other's arms in my bed. I toss and turn in my sleep, so sometimes during the night, I would end up outside of his arms with my back turned towards him. I stirred in my sleep a little and then I turned to wrap my arms around Laron. I felt something near me, so I opened my eyes. Paris was standing right by my bed, in the dark, dressed in all black, with a gun pointed at Laron. She was standing silently with the evilest scowl on her face.

I jumped and yelled, "Oh my God!"

Paris didn't flinch, but my yell made Laron Jerk awake.

"Wha- Oh shit! Paris?" he yelled.

"Surprise mutha fucka." Paris said.

"What are you doing here? How did you get in here?" Laron asked.

"Never underestimate a bitch that can pick a lock. You might want to put a chain on the door when you're out creeping on your wife. What are you doing here? I thought you were supposed to be in New York. That's what you told me, right?"

She slowly moved closer to him pressing the gun into his chest. I watched quietly with fear in my eyes and my cover pulled over my naked body. I don't know why I was covering up. It wasn't like she had never seen me naked. I guess it made me feel protected from her gun.

"Cool out Paris." he said.

"I'm supposed to be cool when my husband is in another woman's bed. The woman that you told me that we were done with?"

"What?" I asked. My face immediately frowned.

"Yes." Paris said to me without looking at me. She had her eyes on Laron and the gun in his chest.

"Paris baby you are tripping right now."

"You have been lying to me, and you really thought that I wouldn't find out?"

She stepped back and pointed the gun at me. "And you. Really? You couldn't find your own man. You had to try and steal mine? I knew you were a shady bitch."

I said, Look, I don't have to steal nothing. Laron tell her."

"Baby, stop." he said to Paris.

"Tell her Laron. I didn't steal anything. You came to me."

"I-" Laron was tongue tied.

"You told me that you were getting a divorce." I said.

She pointed the gun back at Laron. "A divorce?! You've been coming home every night to me, telling me that you love me, but we're getting a divorce? Since when? And why didn't I know about this divorce Laron?!"

He was silent.

Paris continued, "You're a fucking liar. I've read everything. All your text messages. I put a GPS tracker on your phone. That is how I found you here, and you thought that you could get away with this."

She cocked the gun and aimed it at me.

I said, "Paris, I swear, I didn't know. I swear."

She pointed the gun back at Laron.

"You had the nerve to go behind my back after promising me that you would never do that."

Tears began streaming down her face. She kept the gun pointed at Laron while she took a cigarette from behind her ear and lit it with a lighter that she had in her pocket. I didn't know that Paris smoked up until that moment. She took a few heavy pulls from the cigarette and blew the smoke in the air as a river as tears continued to flow down her face.

Laron spoke slowly and quietly, "Baby listen, I'm sorry. Ok. Let's just go home and talk about it."

He was nervous, and I was nervous. I didn't know what she was going to do. It looked to me like she planned to kill both of us. I was praying that she was just there to scare him, and we would make it out of my bedroom alive. Paris stood silently smoking the cigarette like it was the last one she was ever going to have. She looked at me and then she looked at Laron, and then she said, "Fuck going home."

POW!

To Be Continued….

Acknowledgements

Thanks to the Creator for giving me this gift and allowing me to share it with everyone reading this book. I didn't grow up thinking that I would be an author, but the day I decided that this is what I wanted to do, I knew that God had pointed me in this direction, and I am forever grateful. I am finally doing something that I love, and I enjoy every minute of it, so I hope that you loved reading this piece of work as much as I loved writing it. Thanks to my family, friends, readers, and supporters for inspiring and encouraging me. I appreciate all of you and hope that you continue take this journey with me. As always, remember to live, laugh, and love. Smooches!

-Nia Rich

Contact

Email: niarichbooks@gmail.com

Connect

Instagram: @authorniarich

Facebook: @authorniar

Twitter: @authorniarich

238 | P a g e